ISOL

CW00833263

FIVE LIVES, ONE NIGHT; ONE CALAMITY, A MILLION NIGHTMARES

ANIKET DAS

To Friends and Family!

Contents

Acknowledgements

I will run out of words if I thank each and everyone resposnsible for the completion of this book. But i do express my sincere gratitude to my friends who have been my pillars in this journey. I owe you so much guys!

Prologue

PURVI

It wasn't going to be an ideal evening. The vibes suggested so. My desperate heart, however, wanted otherwise. It had been a few months since I spent an evening with my brother the way I wanted to. The way every other sister would want to. I wasn't demanding a movie-esque *'ek hazaaro me meri behna hai'* types evening. No, I hate being dramatic. And I made it a habit to stay away from the ones who consume drama like their daily dose of vitamin pills. But even the toughest of hearts need love to survive. After 'THAT INCIDENT' with our parents, Bhaiya had not been in his element. He had resorted to drinking and that too, maintaining an unapologetic streak. I agree with the fact that he lost his family. And losing the ones who care forever can be devastating at times, especially when neither you nor they are ready for it. But he must realize that another part of his family, one who is more closely attached to his heart, is still alive. It was the time when two broken souls should stick together and mend each other. But arrogance made him do funny things. He resorted to materialistic miracles to mend himself. And I was stuck alone, regretting and suffering in equal measures.

While I was lost in pessimistic thoughts, the door creaked open. He was home. I looked at the clock. 7:05, it said, as if mocking me in its own way. I stood up. I had to take my stand. If he was not ready to be the responsible brother my parents wanted him to be, at least I could be a responsible daughter my parents never cared for. I went downstairs to the hall. There he was, resting his butt on one of the wooden chairs of the dining table, hands cupped over his face. He had brought a gift for himself. A glass bottle shaped like a Dettol Antiseptic Liquid with a cap fitting the mouth perfectly, increasing its elegance. 'OLD MONK RUM' was printed on the sticker in white letters. So, he was making progress, deeper into the gallows of self-destruction. He had already made the bar his new home. Now, he was trying the make his home a new bar. I wanted to speak, I wanted to shout, I wanted to scream. But even my own guts knew I wouldn't be able to. I did care for him a lot, but in those preceding months, I was growing more and more scared of him. I love Pratit, but that asshole sitting on the chair, savoring the taste of whatever he consumed and whatever he was going to consume, that asshole, he was definitely not the Pratit I knew.

Hence, I went upstairs to my room. Getting fresh air was an option. Besides, I didn't want to be a thorn in his way of relinquishing the rum he brought. I grabbed my hoodie and went downstairs again. I cast him one final look, to see if he was even aware of my presence. Well, as expected, he wasn't. He was scrubbing the glass mug which was about to taste the first few drops of those golden pearls of the rum.

I stepped out of the house.

It was pitch black outside. The street lights were all out. There was a thunderstorm warning reported by TrueWeather, the most reliable weather forecasting channel at this side of the state. So, electricity had been out in anticipation to that. That's fair enough.

I wanted to jog around the park next street. But that would have taken a lot of fuel out of my tank in a very short time. Also, I wanted to stay out long, simply because

I wanted to avoid staring at his face when I return. So, instead of going to the park, I dared myself to trek the hill in the dark.

I was intimidated at the first sight. It was the same hill I would have trekked a dozen times at least, but never once in the dark. In a bid to add another feather to my cap, I was ready to throw caution into the wind. Without letting my mind scan for second thoughts, I stepped forward, and eventually, upward.

It was difficult to accurately determine the distance since my good sharp eyes were being tested to their peak powers. But, I was sure about one thing from my hard-earned experience. I hadn't even scaled half the distance. Suddenly, I felt something on my face. A drop, a drop of moisture. Was it dew? Well, I had no time to guess. Within seconds, I was being pelted with millions of such drops. It had started to rain. Well, it had started to storm. The wind, grouped with rain and lightning, followed by loud claps of thunder, started a frantic thunderstorm on the lonely hill. I was literally scared to fits. There was no place to hide. There was no place to run. Going forward would have been a waste. Going down was the only option, at a rapid pace. And sprinting downhill was like playing with fire. But again, standing still and letting the lightning burn you to ashes was an even worse idea. Although I had no family, except my brother, which technically meant no family at all, I still had the urge to live. I still had my friends to go to. I still had hoped to improve my relationship with my brother.

It was a risky move, but I preferred to stick to the edge. I learned an important lesson that day. When you keep mocking your fate, a time will come when it gives you a near-death experience. I had that experience that evening.

While sprinting downwards, even though I managed to keep my eyes wide awake, it was still an impossible task to take notice of anything. The persistent rain, coupled with darkness, posed a different challenge altogether. Amidst the chaos, something happened that I feared the most before taking the route down. I lost my footing and stumbled upon a rock. The toughest one, I realized, courtesy of the memory cells. My balance was reduced to absolutely nothing and my body was ready for a free-fall into the abyss. My brother was going to lose the remains of his already depleted family when he was least expecting it. Then, the miracle, that I always found crazy, happened.

A strong arm grabbed my waist just before my feet were going to desert the last traces of grass. He pulled me towards him and I lay flat on the ground, panting, heaving, and crying happy tears. My guardian angel had rescued me from the jaws of death, in the most dramatic fashion possible.

"I was alive, alive to live one more adventure at least."

Oh! Now I regret these words!

CHAPTER ONE

AARUSH

The warm rays of the sun greeted me on a Sunday morning. My skin was half-baked when I realized I had no choice but to wake up and pull down the curtains even if it meant I had to sacrifice my sleep. After taking long, loud yells of frustration, I finally moved out of the bed near the windows. The sky was bright, even the wooly cirrus clouds were not to be seen in the near vicinity.

"Where is the rain when you need it?" I wondered.

Agree or not, it's blissful, yet a somewhat disturbing truth. Blissful in the sense, that it says that we enjoy our cozy sleep the most when it rains in the morning. Disturbing, because more often than not, it rains in the most harmonious way, when we have to leave bed for college or work.

"Good morning early bird! Although it's already 8, since it's a Sunday, I must admit I'm quite taken aback to see you awake at the moment."

It was my mom. She had her ways with sarcastic remarks. In a way, I had grown accustomed to it, managing a feeble smile out of courtesy.

"Good morning mom!" I groaned. Little did she know, the reason behind the miracle she was witnessing in front of her eyes was not due to my sudden awareness regarding my responsibilities, but majorly because the sun decided to say Hello to my cheeks with its radiant arms which were too hot to handle when I was semi-conscious.

"Aarush! There is no point in trying to fool me. I know you very well. You didn't wake up because you wanted to. You woke up because you were made to. Now, whether it was the heat or the light or the sound, I really don't care. All that matters is, now you're awake. Since you're very aware that today I'm making Chicken Biryani, I want you to fetch me Rice, Onions, and Chicken from the market. I have the rest of the ingredients with me. And be quick! Unless you're happy if your lunch is served at 4 PM. Because unlike you, I can't afford idleness. I have other chores to attend to."

She spoke those last words in a hurry and stormed out of the room, holding the mop she was using to clean the house. Besides, she didn't need to be as rude as she wanted to look. No second invitations were required when it came to Biryani. Add to that, the market is located very close to Purvi's flat.

"I may be in for a surprise after all," I thought.

I grabbed a white t-shirt from the wardrobe with 'Fire' printed on it in orange and black letters. It was one of the dozen white t-shirts I owned. White had always been my go-to color when it came to clothes. Not that I looked any better in it. I just admired it. White is a color that depicted purity. And white is used to mark a person's sanity. I had one confusion in my mind though.

"When we use white on a person, is it to mark his sanity or to mask his vulgarity?"

This mystery surrounding the simple color always intrigued me towards it. Hence, white it was. "Oh, did I mention that Purvi once told me I look good in white?"

I grabbed the keys to my black-colored Hero Maestro from the hook attached to the wall in the hall. No, I didn't own a white vehicle. It's too difficult to keep it clean and sometimes we need to respect logic and keep emotions aside. I didn't own a white vehicle because I knew I would be unable to maintain it. And I didn't want to put additional burden on mom. "Also, did I tell you that Purvi owns a black-colored Honda Activa?"

The market was unusually quiet that day. It was a Sunday, I was expecting a heavy hocus-pocus, at least in the veggies section. But no, it seemed like a normal day. Perhaps, people were still reeling from the effects of the storm that hit the city last week. But then I immediately put that thought away. I didn't want to remember that thunderstorm. It was gone for good. It was terrible, all right, but it affected me in more ways than one. It shook me from within. It took a lot away from me, and the reminiscent of what it had left was even more terrible to bear than the uprooted trees, the shambled poles and the shaken thatches. A storm at this part of the state was not uncommon. I grew up watching lots of them, pelting down the roof of my house. I had my dad with me back then. He used to tell me stories about storms destroying lives and livelihoods. But since he left, storms had evolved. They not only targeted lives, but also souls.

In no time, I had the rice and onions with me. I wanted to stay a little longer, expecting Purvi to arrive anytime soon. But I already had a habit of counting my chickens before they were hatched. And I didn't want to worsen it any further into 'counting my kids before marriage'. I moved to the chicken shop.

Unfortunately, an empty market didn't promise an empty chicken shop. I lived in a locality where people will eat chicken on Sunday even during a war. A thunderstorm was just a fluke. There was an infinitely long queue in front of the most preferred chicken shop in the local market. "Fresh and Crisp Chicken Parlor", was its name. I stood in the queue, waiting for my turn. Before I could realise, I felt a tap on my shoulder. I turned around to see a familiar face.

"Aarush!! Bro!! Wassup!! Is Aunty making Biryani today? Am I invited or not?"

It was Nadeesh. Our class representative. He was a nice, amiable guy. Often overestimates himself, but in a good way, a leader should learn how to lead from the front. And Nadeesh had the ideal template that a representative is expected to follow.

"Hey bro! All good! Yeah, yeah why not? I'll be waiting for ya"

He returned my smile and gave me a playful jab.

"They call this chicken parlor. How cute na?" Nadeesh asked.

"How barbaric", I thought.

"You take a chick out of its artificial home, you slit its wind-pipe mercilessly and wait for all the blood to flow out. Then you remove its appendages including the beautiful wings. Then you chop down the bones and sometimes, the liver too, into small pieces. After doing this, you still have the audacity to name these insane theatrics as 'parlor'. But who are we to blame? We eat this, we gulp down the gravy, we smash down the flesh, and we bite down the bones too."

Of course, I didn't say any of these to him. I just smiled back and replied, "Indeed, it's a unique name".

We chit-chatted for a while and the went our own ways after collecting our respective bags.

I still had a few minutes before my scheduled time to reach home. The thought of taking the alternative route, which ran by Purvi's house, sprang up in my mind. I made up my mind to give it a try at least. The image of seeing the face of the girl I liked so much, lightened up my mood instantly.

When I finally reached her house, there was no sign of life. It was just a metaphor. They were still sleeping. She and her brother. I was early to the market, that's why I missed her. Knowing I had to give up on my hopes, at least for that day, I started to turn the ignition on. But just before I could do that, I felt another tap on my shoulder. I turned around, this time in an irritated sort of way. I saw another familiar face. This time, however, I was nervous and caught red-handed.

"What the hell are you doing here?"

"OH SHIT!" I yelled quietly, to myself.

CHAPTER TWO

LILY

He was sweating, it was clearly evident on his transfixed face. Was it just because of the heat? No, that would just be a blatant excuse. He had no business here, sneaking up on my best friend's house like some lunatic stalker. These introverts, I tell you, are insanely creepy, at least from my perspective. But Aarush? He seemed sort of nice to me in a way. Nicer, than the rest of the guys in my class, to put it in a better way. Now, clouds were being formed over my own perceptions. Did I rate him low? Was he more cunning than what I actually thought of him?

Fortunately, for God's sake, he decided to speak for himself and clear my dilemma.

"Hey, Lily! Nice to see you! No, I was just returning home, from the market, you see."

He pointed to a few bags, one hanging from the left handle of his scooter, and a couple hanging down the hook. He might have a point. This road usually remained very quiet and away from the regular hubbub. A tempting road to choose for the ones in a hurry.

"Some problem with this old horse, so I had to stop here for a bit."

He rubbed a finger over his nose, indicating his awkwardness. When I caught sight of him, he was trying to turn his ignition and was about to leave. So, he had a lot in the truth's favor. I didn't need to cross-examine him anymore, not that I needed to in the first place. However, it had become quite an irksome habit of mine over the last few years, to bombard people with unnecessary questions and make them feel awkward. Some would hesitatingly answer because they feared my dad. Some would give me 'Mind-your-own-business' kind of looks and would carry on with their activities. These were the two categories of people. Aarush, however, belonged to a different category altogether. Neither did he want to be in my dad's good looks, nor did he give me any 'fuck-off' kind of gesture. He answered my questions because he wanted to. He was a nice fellow, and I would rather believe my eyes if I'll ever see a cow with 6 legs, but I'll never believe someone's mouth who'll tell me that Aarush is rude, or had been rude to him even once. Guys like him, they just don't know the definition of being rude, forget the expression.

I realized I had been keeping him waiting for a long time, without much speech from either side. I bade him farewell.

"Chill bud! I was just pulling your leg. Bubbye! See ya tomorrow at school."

"Yeah, sure! Tata! See ya!"

As if waiting for his cue to leave, he sped off within a fraction of a second.

I took a deep sigh and stepped into the entrance of Purvi's house. I rang the doorbell.

No answer. As expected.

I rang it three more times. Finally, a soft grunt came out.

"Ya-Ya! Coming! Hold it man!"

It was the voice of a guy. That indicated either Pratit or.......

I didn't have much time to figure it out. There he was, standing right in front of me. Bare-chested and grinning from side to side, showing his sparkling white teeth and adjusting his shorts up to his waist. His hair was messy and his eyes were red. He didn't have a good sleep, as it seemed. Or maybe he did, just that his sleep wasn't complete.

"Oh, hey Lily! Wasn't expecting you at this time of the day here, ya-ya?"

He had his disgusting smile plastered to his charming face. He distinctively smelt of booze.

"Well, I could say the same about you, Siddharth, ya-ya?"

He gave loud, bursting laughter. He was probably better off smiling.

"Oh, common Lils! Let's keep it Sidd na... We've been mates for over a year. Full names seem like a formality now."

He hadn't recovered completely from the effects of the alcohol. But at least he was in his senses.

"Yeah, fine by me. Now, in case you missed it, I'm here to meet my best 'mate', Purvi. And at the moment, your graceful torso is blocking my way."

"Ah! I'll take it as a compliment babe! But, in case youuuu missed it, I answered the bell, and not her. So, boo is sleeping. And I'm sorry but I can't allow you to enter her dreamland with me."

"Boo? Seriously? And don't fucking call me babe again or I'll chop your head off."

I was serious. I hated this guy. And the hatred had spread through my blood and marrows. Did I hate him for his intimacy with my best friend? Maybe, yes. But that wasn't all. In fact, that didn't matter much at all. He was just a complete bitch, bit-by-bit, piece-by-piece. An arrogant show-off and wanna-be charmer. Maybe he wasn't as terrible as Nadeesh, but Siddharth didn't fit the definition of 'decent guy' either.

"Oh, Lils! The amount of effort you put towards maintaining your shape. If you can put even half of that towards maintaining your temper, you would do a world of good to yourself."

He uttered these shameless words gleefully and burst into yet another fit of laughter. If not for the alcohol, he would have received a mouthful of abuse from me. Since he was under its influence, I decided to give my fist a try instead and turn those sparkling white chicklets into dark red withered pebbles. Just when I raised my fist to punch him hard in the face, his so-called 'boo' intervened.

"Stop it guys! Why are you fighting like kids? Sidd! Go inside! I'll be there in a few minutes. And please wash your face and take some mint or lime or whatever you find. You smell like shit boo!"

Boo? Again? I never expected Purvi to lower her standards to this level. Love is blind, I was well aware. But to be able to experience it practically in the case of your own best friend; goodness me! I'm so fuckin blessed!

"Ya-ya! Anything for you boo!"

Siddharth raised his hand and smiled to imitate the pledge we used to take in our school and quietly went inside. It was good to see, that he had some limits to his tomfoolery, especially with Purvi around.

"Hey, Lils! I'm really sorry on his behalf. You know how he is. Reckless at times, kind of a chipmunk during others. So, just ignore him. He's actually a good person at heart. Try spending some time with him, you'll know too."

"Spending time with Siddharth? No thanks Purvi, it is an offer I would reject without a second thought. I'll prefer chewing all bitter pills at once instead of chewing down his dumbass jokes."

This time, we both shared a laugh. Unlike Siddharth, we both shared the same sense of humor.

"Anyway, leave all that. I wasn't expecting you today. Everything all right?"

"Oh yes, all good. I just wanted the latest edition of the college magazine. You have it?"

It was the partial truth. I didn't like spending time at home, not anymore. Especially after my dad's 4th marriage. I pleaded with mom to move away, to leave that man. But she never listened, never listens even now. How could she be fine, sharing the same roof with 4 other women romantically involved with her own husband? Being the eldest daughter, I was always treated like a princess, but my mom, being the first wife, had always been denied her basic rights. How ironical!

"Oh yes yes! I have it. Wait a minute. I'll be back in a flash."

She was true to her words. Although I was ready to wait for an eternity, she came back in the blink of an eye. She gave me a warm hug and bade me a sweet bubbye. She didn't invite me in. Because another person, who held much more importance in her life than me, was waiting inside to devour her in his arms.

I didn't object. I left quietly. Back to the palace of torments. Back to a sort of brothel, which unfortunately happened to be my home. Behind this adamant, blunt face with a heart of stone, there existed a soul which was yearning for what Purvi had. Money can't buy love. Nor can power. And for a girl like me, who tried to take pride in her ego; we can't afford the luxury of love.

CHAPTER THREE

SIDDHARTH

What's the most wonderful thing about youth? Rather, what's the most wonderful thing about being an adult? Oops, second most wonderful thing, I mean. Because, you see, not being questioned on drinking still comes first. Let me bequest myself with the opportunity to answer this.

The most wonderful thing about being an adult, after the obvious benefits of drinking, is 'the ability to blame everything on luck'.

Don't judge me for being insensitive. I bet, you, your kins, or anybody whose face you somehow happen to remember, has often taken the route of luck as an excuse for his failures. There are a seldom few who believe they are lucky to be living as an adult, despite being burdened with responsibilities and hammered down with failures. With immense pride, I can put my hand up and appreciate the fact that I belong to those seldom few.

When I returned to my hostel on Monday, after spending the entire weekend with Purvi at her house, the superintendent was absent. Aww! My dear old supri. He used me as an ideal example for his kids to follow. In his eyes, I was Mr.Perfect. Although nobody is perfect, as you would have said in your mind by now, I'm definitely the closest guy to what being perfect looks like. However, after my relationship, I barely used to remain in hostel. Supri didn't like to intrude, but he seemed suspicious. I didn't care actually. I just had to make sure that Purvi remained out of his sight.

His absence enabled me to take the front gate instead of creeping through the small hole in the back fence. I had Daman to thank. I could not have asked for a better best buddy in my life. He could even take a bullet for me, let alone Supri's words. A lazy-ass he has, have to accept it, but his heart and brain, both remained on fire all the time. My parents rarely call me, courtesy of Daman himself. He had literally won the hearts of my entire family. He had a very calm head over his shoulders. His responsibility, well, that's beyond his years.

I stepped inside the white-tiled room which happened to me my very own. Daman was still sleeping, by the window. He preferred that. I took the one bed by the door. You can't expect a lazy ass to answer the door every time. So, better this way. For the first time in my entire life, I was so happy even when he was sleeping soundly. The room was left untidy, the shelves looked like the crevices of some ancient cave. The water bottles were all empty. The clothes were scattered inside the bag, yet to be deposited in the laundry. I used to do all these, while he kept snoring. That often brought the worst of the furies out of me, yet I kept mum. I had a habit of pasting my smile on my face even when I was on the extremity of my wrath. Take the example of Sunday morning. That Lily bitch stood on the verandah of my girlfriend, hurling a mouthful of abuse at me. She even raised a fist to punch me. Oh, I would like to see her try it once! What did she think? I was drunk, and that's why I kept smiling? Hell No! I kept my smile intact only because Purvi cares about her so much.

Anyway, back to our concerned scenario. Any other day, I would have loved to lift Daman out of his bed and toss him through the window. But that day, he certainly saved my ass from being humiliated. I would have returned on Sunday itself. Late night, yes, but I don't have any sort of fear of ghosts or evil spirits or any hypothetical being with a peek-a-boo sound. The only thing I'm afraid of is humiliation. Just when I was about to pack my things, ignoring Purvi's pleading requests to stay, Daman called me and told me that Supri was staying in the hostel for the night. He would leave early on Monday. Lo and behold! Just one masterstroke from Daman saved four asses that day. Mine, His, Purvi's, and Supri's. Or else, he would have received a thorough scolding from the dean.

So, Daman deserved a good sleep, for his presence of awareness in the crunch situation. I cleaned the room and the shelves, filled the bottles, and deposited the laundry bag. Just when I was applying gel to my hair, as a final step of getting ready for college, he woke up.

"Mmmmmmm.... Oh, hey Sidd! When did you arrive?

He was rubbing his eyes and still trying to make sense of a dream he probably saw in his sleep. He belonged to a different section and they didn't have morning classes on Monday.

"Hey, Daman! Thanks for the help, man! You literally saved my ass."

"Our asses", he corrected.

We shared a casual laugh.

"Bdw, good morning! I'm sorry we don't have time for pleasantries. I'm getting late. See you at lunch."

"Yeah sure, TTYL"

We exchanged a smile and I sped off the road with my bike.

Well, a clear-cut advantage of staying away from home. There is freedom, lots of it. I bet I wouldn't have got this bike had I stayed at home or somewhere near to it.

The college was 5 km away from my hostel. I was late, I knew it. The college was quiet, which suggested that lectures had already started. I parked my bike at my preferred parking spot and ran towards Lecture Hall-1. I was huffing and puffing by the time I reached the hall. The professors were staring at my face in disgust on the way. 'Argh! Things you do for love'.

I knocked on the door, as softly as I could. When there was no answer, I knocked frantically. A person opened it, and he was not a professor. A sense of relief flowed down my veins to calm the adrenaline rush. It was Nadeesh.

"Hello, Sidd! I'm not surprised you're late. You must have endured a sleepless night."

He winked toward the whole class and Purvi blushed. It was getting more awkward for me.

I somehow saved myself from the embarrassment and climbed the gallery to bench number 5, where Lily and Purvi were sitting. I sat on Purvi's right, while she was sitting in the middle of the three-student bench.

"My god Siddharth! You're panting! Are you alright?"

Thankfully, someone noticed.

"Ya-Ya boo! I'm alright. As far as my panting is concerned, ask someone who had to climb two floors via the stairs at a lightning-fast pace. But as it turns out, I'm not late after all."

"Aww! How thoughtful of you to start from your hostel late and then make up for it by heaving your way through the building. Anyway, your efforts are wasted since our first class has been canceled." Lily interrupted, in her usual fashion.

"What? Canceled? Really Boo?" I turned towards Purvi.

"Yes! Prof.Mishra is absent today." She answered while wiping down my sweat with her handkerchief.

"I didn't have my breakfast. I was about to leave when Nadeesh stopped us midway. He said he has something important to share. I wonder what's that going to be. AS IF WE CARE." Lily asserted her dominance once more.

"Lily! Nobody fucking needs you to care!"

I wanted to yell. But I couldn't. Yet again, I kept that ever-lasting smile on my face.

Hostel life is not a bed of roses. When you stay away from home, you can't afford to start a fight with the locals. Especially when the local is the daughter of a politician.

CHAPTER FOUR

NADEESH

This podium. It was like my regular desk. I had become quite used to standing on it. For the first few days of my tenure as the CR, the mere sight of this podium made me nervous. It took me quite a good deal of dedication, coupled with my passion, to make myself worthy of the title. I used to sneak into the campus during the evening hours when trespassing was strictly prohibited. More often than not, I found the lecture halls unlocked. This casual behavior by the security guard granted me the freedom to sneak into one of them and conduct a thorough rehearsal standing on the podium and speaking in front of an empty audience. I made sure not to speak too loudly, otherwise, the dozed off guard would have woken up. I was envious of the professors who had mastered the art of maintaining an eye-contact with almost every single student at fragmented moments. But now, as I stood on the podium, for the umpteenth time, growing with confidence at every single attempt, I was able to replicate their aura. My eyes were able to scan throughout the class, landing on every intriguing subject which caught my attention. I was starting to enjoy the power of the podium.

As usual, Lily was busy bickering between the two love birds, Sidd and Purvi. She did catch my attention first. Even in a crowd of hundred people, one could easily identify Lily. Not because of her extravagant looks, but for her displeased expressions. She wore a sunken face, vibrant, but in a negative way. She was beautiful, I'll give her that. But she was like that annoying girl in every class who found a problem even with the basic laws of nature. Imagine you're roaming outside, and it starts to pour down heavily. You, me, or anybody else will try to run frantically in search of shelter. But Lily? She'll stand right at the center of the road and scream at the clouds overhead for their unpredictable behavior and ultimately, she'll curse nature for her unfair punishment.

As far as her bickering was considered, it didn't involve any rocket science to decode what she was trying to suggest. Even amidst the ruckus of the class, her voice clearly stood out. She was bitching against me, right in front of my eyes. I heard her taking my name once while telling something to Sidd. It didn't matter to me anyway. We both hated each other. Our fathers hated each other. We were pretty happy with that.

Purvi was listening intently to whatever her boyfriend was filling her ears with. It did bother Lily, to see her possession being owned by someone else. I couldn't help but smile widely.

The A³ gang (Ananya, Akriti, Abhishikta), was busy in some sort of trio-sketching. It was in the infant stage, but by the looks of it, it would turn out to be a beautiful artwork. The last benchers, Bhavna, her boyfriend Drishant, and their friend Prasidh, the usual *kabab me haddi* kind of guy, kept themselves occupied with cigarettes. As far as Aarush was concerned, he was sitting on the front bench, quietly devouring all the knowledge from an encyclopedia.

As soon as my surveillance was completed, I thumped hard on the table fixed to the podium. Immediately, all the eyes were fixed on me. Yet another trick I learned from the professors. They were waiting for me to announce whatever I had in my mind. Some looked excited, unable to hold their impulses. Some were turning impatient. There were contrasting emotions on their faces. I decided to break the suspense.

"Guys! Let me keep this quick and short. The Winter season is coming to an end. Soon, we'll be embracing the freshness of the spring. Unfortunately, freshness is the only thing we'll be able to embrace. Enjoyment will abandon us soon. Our end-term exams are starting from 15th of next month. Hence, it's my duty as the CR to bring this topic to the table. Let's go on a trip this Sunday. The weather looks perfect as of now. Besides, I have a wonderful destination in mind. Suits this kind of weather perfectly."

There was a loud cheer from my mates. Sidd was the noisiest of all. Even Aarush started to hoot. But what surprised me most was Lily's reaction. She was clapping enthusiastically. I didn't know whether it was genuine or fake. But at least she had the courtesy to go with the flow.

"The location is Madhyasthayi Island. All of you must be aware of it. 200 km from here, a small island, extremely small in fact. Not much far from the shore, around 15-20 km. Yes, there might be a lot of tourists but there are no inhabitants. No shops or guesthouses either. So, a perfect way to shake a hand with nature itself. Now, I have laid down my proposals. The ultimate decision lies in your hands guys."

Again. There was a loud chorus of cheers. Everyone appreciated the idea, including the most obnoxious ones. However, just our decision counted to nothing. We needed permission from the college authorities. And getting a hand-written letter of acceptance from the stubborn dean wasn't going to be easy. But again, as a CR, I couldn't afford to be out of ideas. I knew just the solution.

"Okay guys! I'm really thankful for your appreciation. I'm extremely glad you liked my idea. I didn't expect such full-fledged support. But now that I can see the result of my decision, I can proudly say that I was right to choose Madhyasthayi as the spot. However, there is one small problem. THE DEAN."

Soon, the cheers were turned to boos. But even after that, they were smiling. They knew I had something in mind. They had their faith in me. A leader wouldn't ask for anything more than the faith of his people. My father told me that once. He will be proud of me if he sees such a commotion in my favor. Especially because he himself had never tasted the power of ruling as a politician. Lily's father had that privilege.

"So, we need to convince our dean. And it's not going to be easy. My grades are pretty good. But they're not good enough to leave a lasting impression on the dean. We must select the face of this college. The topper of this college. The future of this college."

"It's Aarush." Sidd blurted out.

Everyone shouted in chorus. "Aarush! Aarush! Aarush!"

"Whoa Whoa! Wait a second guys. Yes, Aarush is the topper. But he's a guy. We need someone who the dean likes. Someone for whom the dean has a very soft corner in his heart. Not to forget, the dean himself adjudged her as his favorite student. I'm sure he won't deny her request." I finally broke the suspense.

Everybody's gaze shifted towards the 5th bench. Sidd's and Lily's eyes lit up. There were more cheers, louder this time.

"You mean.... I?"

"Yes Purvi! You! You're one of the toppers and the dean's favorite. You will be our savior today. Accompany me."

CHAPTER FIVE

PURVI

The knight in the shining armor. The girl is on a noble mission. That's how honorable I was feeling. However, I was well aware that this feeling wasn't going to last long. All the honor would turn into misery the moment I set foot inside the dean's chamber. But everyone was so excited as if their spirits had been rejuvenated in some way. I just couldn't say NO to terminate their enthusiasm then and there itself. To be honest, even I wanted to go on that trip. Away from my house and Pratit, since I was starting to feel claustrophobic in my own house. A change of scenery was going to do a world of good, I was damn sure about that.

As we were walking, the corridor seemed quieter than normal, mirroring our own fear. Nadeesh looked confident, but his only job was to escort. I had to deliver the Coup de Grace. The dean would certainly be pleased to see me at his office. But would he be ready to hear those words from my mouth? Would he forgive me if I say something out of context? In the most *un-Purvi* way? Could I even forgive myself? I had been a victim of overthinking ever since I started to coordinate with my brain. When my father bought me a bicycle, I wasn't just afraid that I would fall multiple times. I was afraid that I would break my neck and die and land up in hell and there won't be any cartoons to suffice my hunger for them. When a girl can see the picture of hell on the face of just a simple bicycle, imagine the reach of her vivid imagination. What she might witness on the dean's face.

"Are you sure this is a good idea?" I couldn't restrict my instincts any longer.

Nadeesh turned back, giving me a surprised look. He wasn't expecting a protest from my side, especially when we were a few steps away from our destination. Soon, the shock turned into a smile. Typical Nadeesh!

He turned around and kept walking as if it was just a casual question. How can people take things so lightly? I might scowl at such an approach to handling things. But, deep down, I wanted to be like them.

Nadeesh finally spoke.

"Purvi! Do you remember the fresher's day?"

A question that was completely out of the blue. I wore a clueless look, but I answered nevertheless.

"Yes! Of course! How can I even forget the embarrassment? Why? What happened?"

"Do you remember what the seniors told about you?"

There comes the killer blow. I understood where he was trying to go. But if he really wanted to bring that topic on the table, he could have chosen a different day. I never understood his admiration for seniors. Not only him, even Sidd was fond of our seniors. I just couldn't see the reason behind such unconditional affection. Was I being judgmental in rating them bad? Or was I brutally honest about them which Sidd and Nadeesh couldn't afford to be?

"Yes, I remember! They said, 'Purvi! You're the eye-candy of this college!' If that was your attempt of boosting my confidence, I must admit you have a lot of area to cover as far as your motivational skills are concerned."

At this, he grinned widely.

"Oh Purvi! No, that's not my point. I just wanted to show how highly people speak of you. You're a darling of this college. You're a darling of the dean. As a student, I mean. So, if you request our dean for the trip, consider it approved. I admire your selflessness to let go of your topper ego and work for a mass cause. In fact, you never had any ego. Unlike Aarush. He is a ball of ego. That's why I chose you over him. He has never done anything for anybody but himself. We've already come a long way ahead. We can't turn back now. At least, I can't turn back. So, tell me Purvi. You want to do this or not?"

Aarush was an introvert. He just didn't prefer company. That didn't mean he was egositic. I didn't say anything though. It was beyond my abilities to fight with adamant representatives. I reluctantly agreed to the proposal and we moved ahead. Finally, we standing right outside the door to his chamber. Just a knock away from our appointment with doom. I was able to picture hell again. The dean would rusticate me from the college. My brother would discard me from the house. I would have no place to live in, no food to eat. I would die out of starvation and cold. My vivid imagination ultimately landed up in hell again. This time though, it was interrupted by a soft knock on the door by Nadeesh. I brushed everything aside and composed myself for the grand showdown that awaited us.

"Come in!"

We stepped inside.

It was my second time inside his chamber in two years. The first one was last year for the exact same reason. I wasn't feeling much nervous back then. Because we were ten last time. This time, we were only 2. And only I was supposed to do the talking.

"Arey Purvi! Good morning! How are you?" The dean was genuinely happy to see me.

He was sitting on his usual high-gait chair. It looked more like a gaming chair without lights. He was a tall man. It would have been difficult to find a chair with a headrest as tall as this. Inevitably, they had to go for this one. Their only other alternative was a salon chair.

The photo-frames of many ex-deans, hanging on the wall, greeted me with their smiles. Some, with their frowns. They couldn't wait for me to begin. They couldn't wait for me to get myself expelled.

"Good morning, Sir! I'm fine Sir! What about you?"

I didn't have the luxury of time to spread out the pleasantries. But I was searching for the right delivery to hit a sixer.

"Oh yes my child! I'm pretty well myself! How are your studies going? Your exams are due next month. I hope you're preparing well"

There we go. A delivery right into my swinging arc.

"Yes, Sir I...."

"Common Purvi! Cut the crap already!" Nadeesh whispered in my ears.

"Yes, Sir I... About that. As you know we're having our exams from next month. And this year we haven't been able to go on a trip. Last year was so fun. This year has been very mundane for us. We only have a couple of years left. If we exclude our final year, this could very well be the penultimate chance for us to enjoy a trip. So, we've come to request you to allow us to organize a trip for our section to Madhyasthayi Island. Sir please?"

These words. It seemed like they were brewing inside me for a long time and I was finally able to throw up. My confidence did have an impact on dean. He looked impressed. Nadeesh? He looked jubilant.

"Ah! You kids! You always delve your minds into fictional serials and movies. This generation is being swayed away from reality." He put his hand on his forehead and shook his head. He continued.

"Let me show you something."

He opened the drawer of his desk and produced a black colored TV remote. He switched on the TV, which was present in his chamber and navigated to 'NewsToday' channel.

There were discussions regarding the upcoming elections. Some renowned politicians were not granted any tickets from their respective party leaders. This was going to create quite a stir during the rallies, which were due from next day onwards. I looked at Nadeesh. His eyes were filled with shock, which soon turned into disappointment. I thought perhaps one of his close relatives was denied a ticket. But soon he turned towards me and pointed his finger towards the lower section of the channel where headlines were getting displayed. I understood immediately. And soon, my face reciprocated his own. Utterly disappointed.

"Cyclone warning at the eastern inland districts. All inhabitants are advised not to venture out of their houses. Wind speed predicted at around 200 km/h. This is predicted to be one of the most devastating cyclones ever. Landfall expected during the late hours of 27th January."

The dean read the above lines again and again, to remind us of our negligence. 27h Jan, the day when our trip was supposed to take place. All blown away into a whirlwind. It's over. With nothing but defeat in our minds, we stepped out. Neither of us talked a word on our way back. Nadeesh knew he had to take the responsibility. The responsibility of killing everyone's excitement. The job of defeating everyone else. But the one who was defeated in the worst way possible; It wasn't Nadeesh. It was me!

CHAPTER SIX

LILY

Should I call her? But why? Moreover, how the hell was I going to console her? It wasn't her fault that the trip was canceled. But Purvi being Purvi had overthought herself into a fit of depression. I wasn't happy, don't take me wrong. Just like everybody else, I wanted to get out of my house into a more serene atmosphere. Now I'm stuck again, inside the gallows of mental torture. But even in this defeat, there was a personal victory for me. The face that Nadeesh wore while explaining his disastrous meeting with the dean was one I would savor for a long time. There was no longer the feeling of pride and ego in his voice. There was despair and exhaustion. He had failed us! Unapologetically.

I even clicked his photo to keep it with me. There was something evil about this activity of mine. I wanted to be evil. I wanted to show him what a heartless little bitch I could be. But somewhere deep down, I felt bad for him. I felt sympathy arising out from the crevices of my heart of stone. I felt he needed somebody. Purvi had Siddharth. But Nadeesh? He had to wipe his tears himself. I didn't mean to wipe his tears but at least I could try to make them stop. I had picked up my phone to call Purvi, to talk to her so that she would feel better. But I decided against it. I didn't want to disturb her intimate moments with her boyfriend.

Instead, I decided to call Nadeesh.

He picked the call up after a couple of beeps.

"Hey, Lily." His voice sounded bitter. Perhaps he was expecting a fair number of taunts. Well, not this time.

"Hi, Nadeesh!". I tried to assess my own voice this time. It was quivering. Was I nervous? Not a chance! Lily never gets nervous. Besides, why would I feel nervous while talking to someone I despise. These mere words of self-confidence fell on deaf ears. My voice refused to stop quivering. Add to that, my pulse was rising. I.... I was nervous after all!

"Hi, Nadeesh! I... Lily this side!" Of course, it was me. Why was I even introducing myself?

"Hah! I'm a bloody CR Lily. I'm supposed to save everyone's contact number. *Including yours.* Now, please cut the crap and get to the point. You need any help? Then please just say it. You want to make fun of me? Make it quick. You want me to resign from my post? I was considering the same. So, please. For God's sake tell what you want and Fuck off!"

These words pierced my heart like a needle does to a boll of cotton. A needle shouldn't inflict much damage to a stone. But for the first time in a few goddamn years, I felt my heartbeat racing, and my impulses getting excited. Finally, my heart was behaving normally for once.

"No no! You're mistaken. I'm not here to laugh at your situation. You're as much guilty as everyone else is. You were trying to lift our spirits. And that's the job of a leader. You were down and out. We all were. Yet you maintained your smile and positive aura throughout the entire day. I could easily say it was fake. But you tried. Just like a leader should. Sometimes, leaders get carried away when they get a taste of raw power. They shy away from their basic responsibilities and often tend to ignite their torches out of influence, not out of duty. They want a certain dignity not because it's a privilege, but because it's powerful. You've never been like that. You have a rare quality that only a few leaders possess. It's called RESPECT. I've never seen you use, or rather misuse your power to reap fruits faster than others. In case of achievements, you've lauded us with praises. In case of failures, you've claimed responsibility without any hesitation. The post of CR is both big and small, depending upon the context. But you Nadeesh, we couldn't have asked for someone better than you."

Was I really praising him? Was I admiring him? What was happening to me? Those words.. nobody would believe I said them. Maybe warm blood was starting to flow through my heart.

"Gosh Lily! That was one power-packed pep-talk. But really, thank you so much! I'm feeling much better now. I never expected these words to come from you. Now that they do, I feel much relieved. I'm not trying to woo anyone. But I like to maintain a good relationship with everyone. And yeah, I'm not disappointed or sunken down or anything like that. I've a plan in mind. I just hope everyone agrees."

Strangely, I felt relieved that he didn't sound upset. And this time, his cheerful-self seemed genuine, at least to me.

"That's great news. Besides, Purvi has Siddharth to pamper her. You definitely needed someone to cheer you up. So, I was just repaying your good work."

I couldn't believe I was pampering him. What the hell was this strange feeling? Throughout my life, I ran away from all sorts of emotional attachments. Now, when I should be running, when I should be swaying away from the strings that were attempting to bind us, I felt my feet stuck in quicksand. The quicksand of this strange feeling. It was like a drug which was soothing my ailing heart. Instead of running away, I wanted to stay. I wanted to consume more of this drug. Little did I know, the drug was actually consuming me. But what is this drug? Is it what they call.... No, I better not think about that.

"Thanks Lily! It was really sweet of you. I gotta go! But be sure that you remain online at around 10 PM tonight. I may need your support. Bye."

He disconnected the call. 10 PM? Plan in mind? Need support? What was he trying to refer to? With the trip all but a forgotten dream, was there any backup? Whatever it was, I wanted to be there for him. To give him the support he so badly wanted. If he was indeed planning for a backup to our trip, I'll be the first one to join him. Partly, because I wanted to get out of my house. Secondly, because I wanted to be with him, especially for the happy moments. The hammer had done its job. The heart of stone was finally crushed. It's all flesh now. The longer it stays, the better. I couldn't believe I said these to myself.

CHAPTER SEVEN

SIDDHARTH

My date evening with Purvi was destined to be ruined. Thanks to Nadeesh and his out-of-the-blue plans. I mean, seriously, he couldn't find a better day, rather a better night for his bullshit. His request to remain online at 10 PM was nowhere related to our academic interests. Either he wanted to make amends for his slip-up or he had some other plan in his mind. If the latter was indeed the case, both I and Purvi wished it would be something worth staying online for. A night with each other was obviously too big a sacrifice, especially for us.

I have to admit that Purvi hasn't been herself today. Especially after that visit to the dean's office. Is she carrying the same guilt as Nadeesh? Just when I was about the break this deadlock of silence, she broke it first.

"Boo! I wanted to ask you something. Will you be honest with me? Please?"

She was looking straight into my eyes. There was a light of rejuvenated energy in them. She was adamant. It seemed like she put up a lot of courage and a deep insight before putting up this question. I was getting a bit nervous. But it's Purvi we're talking about. One way or the other, I was bound to submit to her requests.

"Ya-Ya! Sure Boo! Ask away!"

"Tell me! Did you... Umm... Did you... You know... During that Volleyball Tournament... Did you....?'

She was hesitant. I used to believe we had grown so close. I used to believe we could share everything without a second thought. But looking at her hesitation, I was able to draw two conclusions.

Either the conversation we were going to have, was extremely sensitive, or else we had not grown as close as I had thought. As strange it might sound, I wished the latter to be true. But again, luck and I never get along well.

"Okay, Sidd! I don't want to keep beating around the bush. Tell me. During the volleyball tournament last week. Did you kiss a girl?"

There we go! The gates had been opened. The flooding waves of the water had been allowed to come in.

Now, this kiss thing goes a long way back. I've always been good at volleyball. Right from 7th grade, I have been representing my respective educational institutions.

A champion player often attracts a lot of eyes. And when the champion is attractive, he attracts even more eyes. It's not a grand discovery to admit that a lot of those eyes belong to the opposite gender. Such has been the case with me. It isn't tough to woo girls, considering my all-round skills. But one princess, in particular, had managed to woo me back head over heels.

She goes by the name Simran. An exquisite volleyball player herself. Loud-mouthed but equally vocal in her actions. Her smashes are worth watching. She often brings a sense of professionalism with her acrobatic style of play.

We met for the first time during our 7th grade itself. We both won the prestigious Player of the Tournament award, in the boys' and girls' categories respectively. Since then, nobody has been able to pip us from our position. Our skills became the reason for our conversation. The whole majority of our initial days as friends revolved around volleyball. It took quite a few months for both of us to get into our personal lives. We were in our 9th grade when it happened for the first time. Volleyball Tournaments were the only spots where we could meet face to face. She lived in a town which was more than 400 km away from my home. It was definitely not within the limits of a school-going guy to arrange a solo trip that far.

Coming back to the incident, it was the night of the finals. As expected, we ruled the roost and emerged victorious. It had become a custom for the organizers to etch our names on the trophies even before the official final verdict. After the presentation ceremony, we found a quiet place to sit and talk. We were in our mid-teens. We just won a trophy. The hormones were running high. The emotions were running high. We had grown pretty close by then. We flirted occasionally on Facebook. And then... It just happened. Yeah, we kissed. And it was a long and passionate one. The following year, we took a step further and made out in a room. During our 12th grade, we did something which is considered unacceptable for students of that age. Yes, we did what you're thinking right now. Neither of us was really serious about any sort of relationship. We often searched for worldly pleasures. And we found them within each other. Literally, inside each other. I didn't love her. She didn't love me either. Not even a bit. All we craved for was each other's physical bodies. That's it. I agree. Purvi isn't the first girl I've kissed. And she's certainly not the last. But my love lies with her. Don't take me wrong. That's me. That's we. Sidd and Simi are just two variants of each other. Carbon copies as far as our personalities are concerned. And this past week, we did it again. Unapologetically. We loved the experience. What's so wrong in that?

Purvi snapped her fingers in front of my eyes to bring me back to the present.

"What? No boo! I didn't kiss anybody. You must be crazy to even think like that."

Common guys! You expected me to tell her the truth? Would you have told even an ounce of truth if you were in my place? Be honest. No, right? So, don't judge me for fucking my way around. It doesn't matter whether you do it with two girls at a time or twenty. When it's more than one, you are ethically wrong. That's what the society wants you to believe. And me? I'm much of a rebel myself.

Purvi didn't put any questions after that. I dropped her home and went straight into my room. The date night wasn't as good as I expected. Her reaction to my answer wasn't as bad as I expected. Little did I know, the seeds of doubt were planted in her mind after my denial of the acquisition that I kissed Simran. Things were never same after that.

CHAPTER EIGHT

PURVI

"The day just keeps getting worse". My heart shrieked out to my soul. As if my faceoff with the dean wasn't enough, Sidd's confident dismissal of the rumors surrounding his alleged affairs with a girl named Simran really caught me out cold. He bashed all the accusations without any hesitation. Was he right? Was I being pranked?

I opened my phone and unlocked it. 9:45 PM, the clock read. I still had 15 mins before the requested commitment by Nadeesh. I opened the gallery and scrolled through the sections. I opened the folder titled 'WhatsApp Images'. It was something I shouldn't have done. But I can't blame myself. When you're in your early twenties, you develop a lot of skills. Some skills make you extremely proud, and some inflict self-doubts upon yourself. 'Overthinking' is one such skill that is associated pretty closely with this age. I don't know whether it's good or bad. But it certainly eats you from the inside.

I selected that photo which was sent was sent by one of Sidd's closest acquaintances. I zoomed in again and again repeatedly to check for any signs which suggested the image was photoshopped. My heart wanted to believe it was photoshopped. However, my mind had other ideas. And perhaps, my mind was right. 100% right. He kissed Simran.

Pictures speak a thousand words. And this pic in particular suggested that the kiss was very passionate. He lied. But why? Was I so bad a partner? Or was I with the wrong person? So many questions. All of them lay unanswered. And when a young mind is piled up with such questions, it often seeks the help of the heart. And at crisis times like these, the heart resorts to the lethal tool of overthinking to either pacify the soul or eat it away. Or both, simultaneously.

I was on the verge of an emotional breakdown. That happens very seldom. I've lived through a lot. I lost my parents. I have an estranged relationship with my brother. Now, the person I trusted the most can't keep his genitals inside his pants. Arghh! I wanted to scream. To let it all out. The frustration of all these years. I wanted to eke out everything then and there itself. But, right during the inception, a notification popped on my screen.

WhatsApp> SEC-A> Nadeesh-> "Guys! All in?"

Okay. It was 10 already. My theatrics can wait. I have something more important to tend to. Important according to our CR. Suddenly a flurry of messages accompanied.

Daman -> "Yo boii! Wassup?"

Drsihant -> "This better be good Nadeesh! I am yet to finish my wine and vomit on Bhavna while making out. So I repeat. This better be important.

Gross. And they call this love. Anyway, I'm not too qualified to comment on love or relationships either. My own relationship is mottled.

Akriti -> "Hello everyone! I'm too excited about this! Common Nadeesh! Don't keep us waiting."

Ananya -> "Me too guys! And I'm getting a gut feeling that the trip might be happening after all."

Prasidh -> We're not here to chit-chat guys. Where is the man of the moment.?"

He's got a point. Everybody already has a plethora of problems to deal with. If Nadeesh is unnecessarily dragging this thing, he's intentionally damaging his own reputation as a good leader.

No messages from Sidd. Not yet. Was he feeling guilty about what he did? He was online though. Was he texting Simran? There you go... Overthinking!

Bhavna-> That's enough Nadeesh! Will you speak or shall we leave?"

Nadeesh -> Whoa! Whoa! Wait, guys... I'm preparing my message in the Notes App. I'll paste it here. Give me a few seconds.

Sid -> Don't worry bro! Take your time! We're here for the night.

I don't know whether it meant it sarcastically or he was serious about it. After all, a whole night text session or God knows what, with Simran sounds very alluring.

Nadeesh -> " So guys!!! As ill-luck would have it, we weren't able to win over the authority regarding our trip. Requesting The Dean time and again would make matters worse. So, in light of the upcoming hectic schedule, I've decided that the trip can't be compromised. We're in our sophomore year and we deserve ti enjoy every bit of it. This college, and this academic career, in particular, is completely unpredictable. So, I was us to live it as long as we have a chance. So, it may sound a bit crazy, but I've decided that the trip shall go as planned. We'll go to Madhyastahi. Together. But the twist lies in the fact that our trip will be unofficial. Nobody shall be responsible for our well-being. The landfall of the cyclone is expected to be on 27th January. We will go on 26th, which coincidentally falls on Sunday. We'll camp there till evening and return by 10 PM. I can assure you that I won't back out of this plan. Even if two people decide to go, I'll be one of them. Okay. Now, the decision with you. Who wants to venture out and who wants to pull out?

He's certainly gone crazy. It's a good thing that he admitted his plan was crazy. Sometimes, being crazy ain't as bad as it sounds. So, I typed my decision straightaway.

Me -> " Sounds good! I'm all in."

Yes! I decided to go. And I didn't instantly regret my decision either. I was ready to do anything to fly out of this claustrophobic environment. Even if that meant putting my own life in jeopardy.

Sidd -> Well, since she's going, it only means one thing. Count me in!

Drishant -> Sorry peeps! Sundays are meant for Netflix and Chill! Count me and Bhavna out of it.

Prasidh -> You're right Nadeesh! Your plan is not only crazy, it's fucking insane. Count me out.

Akriti-> Ooopsyy! Me, Ananya, and Abhishikta are planning to have a sleepover at my house. Besides, our parents won't allow us to go amidst the cyclone news. I'm really sorry. But we're out.

Daman -> Wow! You're indeed a courageous leader Nadeesh! I would have loved to be a part of this trip. But, I've some prior commitments. So, I won't be here on Sunday. But I'll definitely enjoy looking at your pictures and videos. Have a blast, guys!"

Pictures and Videos. What a prick. How ironical he made it sound. It was Daman who sent me Sidd and Simran's kissing photo. I realise that he was trying to protect my self-esteem, but somehow deep down, I didn't want to forgive him. Maybe because I was too blind to notice the shithousery of Sidd.

The status bar showed that Lily was typing something. I was expecting a flurry of abuses. Lily was a ticking time bomb, ready to explode. Nadeesh was her detonator. These two hated each other to the root. Hence Lily was expected to pull out of the trip, but not before humiliating Nadeesh. But...But... But... She silenced us all with her response.

Lily-> The plan sounds great! At least for me. Besides, Nadeesh is right. We deserve to enjoy our sophomore year. So, I'll join.

WHAT THE HELL? I'm not very good at reading or comprehending people maybe.

Aarush -> I'm in.

Ha! Typical Aarush. No non-sense talks. Just a Yes or No. These attributes do make him very adorable though.

Nadeesh -> Alright guys! Thank you so much. So it's Me, Aarush, Lily, Sidd, and Purvi. Okay then. I respect your decisions. I wish everyone the best weekend of their lives. Good Night!

He shouldn't have wished that!

CHAPTER NINE

AARUSH

Informing mom wasn't going to be tough. After Dad passed away, she had been trying her level best to be the best parent possible. And she had done an outstanding job at that. It's never easy to lose your partner and then behave as if everything's normal. I had seen her weeping, multiple times. But every single time, she had done it secretly. In front of me, she had been stoic, an absolute rock would be an understatement. She had persuaded me to hang out with friends and let go of my introverted self. It's not like I haven't tried at all, but maybe I'm just too naïve and brutally honest to make friends. I speak too less, so it's not much of a surprise that I'm a loner. I pride myself on that.

But now I had a purpose. A purpose to defy my personality and break the rules. I wanted to go on that trip. I still had no desire to make a lot of friends though. But I wanted to be with Purvi. Not that she needed me or something like that. I would be happy to maintain my distance from her. I would never invade her space. But to see her, to feel her presence, to feel her soul lingering around the aura of my own soul. That's pleasant, even to think of it. Do you guys call it love? I don't know. Perhaps it's better not to associate such a supreme feeling with paltry names.

"Good morning Aarush! All set for college?" My mom interrupted my train of thoughts.

"Yeah, mom! All set. Good morning. Umm. I had something to tell you."

"Yeah sure.. What is it?"

Her smile widened. Perhaps she was expecting it. No, not the trip in specific. But she was expecting that it was somewhere related to me going out and making friends.

"We have a college trip on the 26th. To Madhyastahi. I'm going. I'll be back by 10 PM."

There was this thing about cyclone. But Mom didn't remain too updated with the news. Perhaps she had no idea about the cyclone. Or she wasn't aware about the date of landfall.

"26th? Seriously? I think I've told you a dozen times that 26th of this month is the 1st anniversary of our cafe. You still forgot about that completely?"

Shhoot! She's right. She did remind me a lot of times. And it escaped my mind. Perhaps I was lost in some thoughts where I shouldn't have. Now, this was a golden opportunity. I wouldn't get a lot of chances to be with Purvi. I couldn't afford to let it go.

"Oops! Sorry Mom! I... I forgot. But common! Even you know that the café is doing splendidly well. In a few months, it's clearly the best in town. So.. I think you don't really need a grand celebration now."

I knew I fucked up. It was too casual from my side. Something I had never associated with me before. Mom needed my help. She would never want to celebrate this landmark alone, without her only family that remained. I was stuck in a dilemma to choose between her and Purvi. The fact that Purvi didn't give a shit about my existence and mom would stay through my thick and thin was supposed to make the decision easier. But it didn't. I was still inclined towards Purvi. They say 'Love is Blind'. I didn't know whether I was in love or not. But I did realise that I was blind. Blind for Purvi. I was struggling for words. But then, Mom showed why mothers have the most selfless hearts in the entire universe.

"It's Okay. I'll manage. Preeti Mausi will be coming for help. So, it won't be a problem."

I couldn't believe my ears. I wished to run upto her and embrace her into a tight hug and scream, "I love you, Mom."

But I was too shy to even speak.

"Thank you mom." I just blurted out these 3 words sans any emotions.

"Go and enjoy. Have fun. But promise me you'll be back by 10 PM."

"I'll be back by 10 PM. I promise Mom. And all the best for the event. I'm sure the customers will love the arrangements and surprises."

She smiled and patted my back.

I made a promise to return sharp by 10. I didn't hug her either. I was sure I would get enough opportunities to fulfil them in the near future. Alas! Some things should never be taken for granted.

CHAPTER TEN

NADEESH

Sharp 6 AM. That's what the instruction was. And that's what they were supposed to follow. But nope. Human beings and time. Find me a better pair of foes. While I was steadying myself on a bench at the railway platform, my dear travelers were nowhere to be seen. You come to think of girls like Lily and Purvi. They have a certain 'Wanderlust' tag on their Instagram bio. Sadly, this lust was yet to teach them the value of time for travel. The train was scheduled for 6:30 AM. But I was well aware of the fact that it would be running at least an hour late. We're talking about The Indian Railways afterall. This careless attitude of arriving to the platform late is often associated with the irresponsible behaviour of railway staffs.

Finally, at least someone from the group decided not to test my patience further. It was Aarush. Someone who would never break the rules. I was kind of expecting him. If there's one person in this whole world who would be on time even to a railway station, it's him.

"Sorry mate! I was a little late to wake up. Hence the delay. Really sorry to keep you waiting."

Aarush and his formalities, ladies and gentlemen.

"Common Aarush! It's absolutely fine. Besides, you can't see quite the commotion here now, can you? And unlike you, they won't be apologetic for getting late. Not as long as they catch the train anyway."

He lets out a deep sigh and sits beside me. I glanced at my watch. 6:45AM, it read. Amidst our chit-chat, the watch reached the mark of 7.

"There they are!!!" Aarush squealed in a delighted done. I looked followed the direction of his fore-finger and I noticed two extremely pretty girls with stylish outfits ready to attend a fashion concert. Seriously, Lily and Purvi gave me vibes of the auditions for the Miss India Title. Yet, they failed to surprise either of us. They always had this thing for makeup. Lily in particular. Be it fests, events or simple athletic meets. Lily made it sure to stand out amidst the crowd. A habit I found extremely showcase-worthy, yet adorable.

While me and Aarush and were inquiring about the how they reached here and about the scheduled plans, the irritating voice of The Railway Lady, as she's fondly called, caught our attention.

"Your attention please! Train number xxxxxxx , Madhyastahi superfast express, will be arriving soon at platform number 5."

That did catch us off guard. We were at platform number 1. Platform number 5 was 4 staircases away. We picked up our baggage and sprinted off.

The girls, with their atrocious attire, obviously found it difficult to sprint fast without tripping. While Purvi grabbed Aarush's hand without hesitation, Lily couldn't approach mine flamboyantly. Ah! Maybe I was too naïve to notice how cute she looks when she's nervous. Without any other choice up my sleeve, I grabbed her hand in mine and we followed Aarush and Purvi at full pace.

We reached our destination in 5 minutes, courtesy of the fairly empty Railway Station. Thanks to the cyclone.

The train was yet to arrive. While we were taking turns to relax our lungs with water, Purvi screamed.

"Oh, Shittt! Sidd!!!"

"You're right Purvi. Sidd is shitt." Lily laughed at her own joke but nobody joined. This was a serious issue. We were able to hear the train's siren from a distance and this a-hole was yet to be found.

"Call him." I suggested. I could have called myself. But Siddharth would definitely prefer her call over mine.

"Thank Goodness he's not switched his phone off," Purvi exclaimed with her phone closely pressed to her ear.

"What the f-? He rejected the call."

That does it. If Siddharth was trying to pull off a publicity stunt to impress us, he had a lot of trouble coming his way. Thankfully though, Aarush calmed our nerves.

"There he is. Hey Sidd! You definitely gave us a panic dude." Aarush shouted something, pointing his finger again. This time, at Siddharth.

It wasn't a full-fledged trip. I agree. It could have been much better. But Siddharth's approach did hurt me. It put a question mark over my dignity as an organizer. He was in shorts. A plain white t-shirt and his hair was a mess. He was wearing slippers we use in the toilet. It was pretty obvious. He woke up late and didn't bother to look at himself even once in the mirror. He didn't look too bad in the attire; he's got heavenly looks after all. But the etiquette in his dressing was missing. And I was pretty certain that throughout the day, the etiquette in his behavior would remain missing as well.

"Speak of the devil, and here he comes. You have no fucking responsibility, idiot. You are late. And I wish you were late for another 10-20 minutes. We would have left without you with zero regrets, dumbass."

Whoa! I was wrong. Lily hasn't changed a lot. Probably it was my perception that she had changed. Or maybe, she did change, albeit, for certain persons.

The train arrived immediately, not letting Lily finish her rant. Fortunately, we didn't have to do much running this time as coach number S-3 was just a few steps away from us. Without further ado, we boarded the train and went to our respective seats. It was supposed to be a short trip. Just a few hours of lifespan, that is what we had granted to this trip. In my gut, there was something else. I felt a strange vibe suggesting that the trip wasn't going to be that short after all.

CHAPTER ELEVEN

PURVI

The trip was supposed to be a distraction. A distraction from my misery. Misery, which was my home. Misery, which was my brother. Misery, which was my life. But this misery refused to let me go. Sidd, who seemed to exude protective vibes every time I was around him, now scared me. I was starting to despise him. I didn't fall in love with Sidd the person. I fell in love with his aura. His positive personality. He was the one who saved me from falling, from a cliff during a thunderstorm. It was a suicide mission, to go trekking in the dark. But he put his own life at risk to pull me right from the edge. It could have been a horrible accident. It was a misfortune. But this specific misfortune changed our fortunes. It brought us closer. I felt like I had finally met the one for me.

Now, when I was starting to believe that I was just in a mirage of desperate expectations, my loyalties with my own soul were clouded with thoughts and doubts.

We reached the Madhyastahi station at around 11 AM. I had been here once before. With my then-alive parents and my then-sane brother. It had been a decade since I last landed here. Not much had changed in these years, or perhaps I was too distracted and upset to notice the minor details. Sidd seemed pretty relaxed during the journey. He even took a relaxing nap for about half an hour or so. Nothing was bothering him. Not even the fact that he shamelessly lied in front of a girl who was ready to devote her life to him.

"Purvi! You, okay? You seem a little off-color since morning."

If there's one person in this entire universe who could sense even the slightest change in my mood, it's Lily. No surprise she instantaneously detected a change in my overall body language.

I wanted to tell her. Tell her the whole thing. Show her the photo. I couldn't afford to trust someone anymore after what happened with Sidd. But somehow, Lily seemed safe. She had always been safe. People have misunderstood her time and again for her blunt attitude. But she's always been real. She didn't fake things. Unlike some people!

"You two! Everything all right there? All good to go?"

Two voices interrupted our conversation. And not a single one of them belonged to Sidd. He was busy clicking selfies. Perhaps he was planning to send them to Simran and God knows who else.

The voices belonged to Nadeesh Aarush. Both of them genuinely looked concerned.

"Yeah! I think Purvi...."

"It's fine guys! Thank you for your concern. But I'm fine. Let's gooooooooooo!!!!!!"

I didn't let Lily complete her sentence. I wanted to tell. But I had to find an appropriate time and place to do that. Not here, especially not when the man in question was busy grinning at the camera.

The Old Town of Madhyastahi was the same as I had last seen it 10 years back. Not a lot had changed. Apart from a few cracks in the buildings and some lichens occupying the monuments. The residents of this town had made it a habit of not adapting themselves too much to the modern world. After all, this town possessed a heritage. A rich culture comprising historically significant art and architecture. Changing to the modern aspect would destroy the landscape. And this place would lose its status as a tourist spot.

The famous Deewar Darwaza of Old Town was a major attraction. It was often found laden with people just like ants around a big mound of candy. That day, it only had 5 visitors. Us. The cyclone was proving to be our ally in fact. The long walls, once belonging to a fortress stretched miles beyond the horizon, or so it seemed. At certain intervals, they had small doors made out of forged iron. These doors served as the entrance and exit of the cavalry as well as the infantry. Hence the name, Deewar Darwaza. The towers just inside the gates housed the artillery.

After having our fair share of time visiting the fortress, which had now become a museum, we marched on towards The New Town of Madhyastahi.

This place was not as breathtaking as Old Town. It just had a lot of shops, where craftsmen from all the 29 states and 9 UTs of India sold their products. Starting from paintings, to pot works, to shawls, to idols. Every state had a unique blend of its art forms. A lot of the shops were closed, owing to the lack of tourists. The overhyped food court of New Town was also closed. Besides, nothing beats the momos made by Aarush's mom which we devoured on the train. There's magic in her hands. It's no surprise that her café became an instant hit in such a small period.

"Alright, guys. I hope you liked Brother Towns. Old Town and New Town of Madhyastahi. Now for the exciting part of our journey. Boating, and visit to the island."

I had completely forgotten about it. The magnum opus of our trip. We went to the shore to see any boats. To be honest, I had expected that our plan of visiting the island and the cave would be foiled due to boatsmen taking precautionary measures against the cyclone. I was almost right about it. But as if The Almighty sensed our desperation, a single boat was present near the shore. He did charge a high price but we were all in. There was enough room for 10 people on the boat. We were just 5. Nadeesh took a seat just near the bow. Lily joined him. They went on with their chatter. Right from the train, throughout the museum, throughout the craft shops, they had been clinging to each other. If something was indeed happening between them, I would rather kill myself. Lily and Nadeesh? That's a whole new brand of Bollywood drama.

I took a seat near Aarush. He was taken aback, his reaction suggested so. But he didn't protest. He maintained an appropriate distance between us and looked around the ocean. I cast a look at Sidd to observe his reactions. Guess what? He wasn't even looking at me. He was making a video, a blog for his YouTube Channel perhaps. There was no network service in this part of the world. Perhaps he was planning to post it later. We didn't talk even once during the journey. This fact was eating me from inside. He looked unfazed by it. Did he truly love me?

Meanwhile, the sky was starting to get overcast. The sun hid behind the clouds. A gentle breeze was starting to flow. If these were early indications of a cyclone, we're screwed.

CHAPTER TWELVE

AARUSH

Things were not looking good. As far as the weather was concerned, it didn't seem like we were still a day away from the landfall of the cyclone. Judging by the air around us, the cyclone felt too close for comfort.

But cyclone was not the only thing bothering me. Things seemed far from right between Purvi and Siddharth. One wouldn't know that just by looking at Sidd. He was his original cool self. But Purvi seemed down and out. Right from the morning, she hadn't been herself. Generally, whenever something happens to anybody, it's always Purvi to cheer him/her up. She was our healer. But a healer often fails to nurse its own wounds. Purvi was facing a similar challenge. Was it my responsibility now? To life her spirits? If it was, I would happily shoulder the burden. But do I even possess the right? After all, I was nothing more than a classmate. Maybe just a friend. Was this trip supposed to change my fate? Only time will tell.

We touched the island shore at around 2 PM. My mom had packed lunch for all of us. So, it wasn't much regret when we witnessed a closed food court back in New Town. Nadeesh was the first to get off the boat, followed by Lily. I and Purvi followed suit. Siddharth was the last, still talking to his followers on IGLive I guess. Nadeesh thanked the boatman and asked him to return for us at 7 PM.

"7? Look at the weather Nadeesh. I don't think it'll be safe for us to be here till 7. We should leave early."

Wee, that's as polite as Lily can get.

"Chill Lily! It's gonna be fine. The weather is just a bit overcast. It's normal at best."

Surprisingly, Lily didn't protest. Incredible!

"Hola Guyss! Sorry I wasn't able to join in. So, we're finally here! Where's the damn cave?"

Finally, Sidd spoke. Not to his cell phone, for a change.

I was expecting Purvi to give an ecstatic reaction since her beloved boyfriend was finally back to his senses. But, no. No change to her gloomy mood.

"Oh, congratulations Sidd! It's really great to know that you don't have a speech impediment as we suspected earlier." At this joke from Lily, everybody burst into laughter. Everybody, excluding Purvi. Now I was starting to get worried.

The island did harbor quite a few rare species of birds. But they were mostly visitors. They came in search of food and went away at the stroke of the dark. As the area occupied by the island was too less, it looked more like a dune rather than an island. The eye-catcher was definitely the cave. It was located just a few meters away from the shore, right at the heart of the island. It was known for sheltering a lot of invaders who came to attack The Kingdom of Madhystahi. While none of them were successful, this cave became a site of historical significance. Buried weapons were preserved inside the caves, worth millions. Nobody has been able to discover a single piece of an artifact to date. Burrowing, digging, etc. were strictly prohibited. There were no guards, but there were cameras. Guarding against any intruder. It was impossible to even reach the island without a legal boat. Forget about entering that cave. While the height of the cave was less than a one-story building, the length wasn't too vast either. What made it stand out were the tablets and inscriptions of the warriors who had stayed there. They had praised this cave for its phenomenal strength. Even in a cyclone-prone area, it had stood rock-solid, having weathered thousands of storms, without crumbling down. We were just hoping it could sustain one more. Just in case....

There wasn't much talking while we explored the cave. Lily was trying her best to cheer Purvi up. Nadeesh was leading the way all alone. And I was stuck with Sidd and his gloating about his knowledge of past events. I'm not much of a history buff myself. But even I could clearly distinguish what events were true and what events were made up by him.

We camped just outside the shore and decided to play volleyball. Team 1 – Sidd and Me. Team 2- Nadeesh, Purvi, and Lily. It did come as a surprise when Purvi rejected Sidd's offer to join our team. Perhaps it was a confirmation that things were definitely ugly between them. But when Sidd gave an 'I-don't-care-attitude', I wasn't surprised. That's him all the time. We won the game, by the way, thanks to Sidd's incredible skills.

In no time, the clock was inching towards 7. All the fun, the plans, the moments, it's over. Moments were supposed to become memories. And memories fade away with time. We could see the boat near the horizon. Just a few minutes more.

What hurt me was the fact that I wasn't able to talk to Purvi much. It was such a good opportunity to at least share our thoughts and beliefs on certain topics. But what hurt me more was the fact that she was upset. And Purvi getting upset is not normal. It was seldom and it was devastating for me. Especially when I wasn't able to do anything about it.

"GUYYYYSSSS!!!!! LOOOOOKKKK!!!"

Lily screamed in horror.

We all looked in the direction of the boat. It was shaking, terribly. The waves paid no respect whatsoever. They were on a rampage. All of a sudden, the hair on our neck stood up, we were having goosebumps. Goosebumps of fear. The wind had started to pick up the pace. It's not a gentle breeze anymore. It was a freaking storm. A very violent one. It was so strong that the sand on the island began to disperse from its place. Ever heard of a desert storm? We were witnessing that on an island. While we busy giving shocked reactions to each other, the waves devoured the boat. Our only way of escaping the island was consumed by the giant ocean in just one single go.

We're definitely screwed.

CHAPTER THIRTEEN

NADEESH

"EVERYONE!! Inside the cave! Hurry up!" We sprinted inside the cave to avoid getting blown away by the strong winds. We were still reeling from what we saw back there. Our escape route was destroyed right in front of our own eyes. If this is the feeling people get before their death, I must admit, it's scarier than death itself.

Back inside, the winds could be heard clearly over our heads. We had no idea what to do. Just praying for something to salvage us out of the deep pit we had fallen into.

"Oh, Shit Shit Shit Shit Shit! We're done! We're finished! Fuck this. We're damned! We're doomed."

Sidd was having a panic attack. And to be honest, nobody could really blame him for that. Here we were, at a completely unknown place. In a completely unknown cave. There were no wild animals, that's for sure. But there could be snakes, lots of them. We needed to calm our nerves and think of something to get our asses off this island. But by the look on everyone's face, it was pretty evident that nobody was ready to talk.

"Yoouuu....gotttt...us....intooo....thisssss"

Sidd was eyeing straight at me. And he was not the carefree version of him we had been accustomed to. His eyes were sparkling. There was no life in his voice. He had given up. The voice seemed to have been transported to his eyes. There was something sinister brewing up inside him. It was quite natural of him to blame me for all this. While the sound of the wind outside the cave was already giving us an eerie vibe of horror, Sidd here had become a persona of some conjured-up spirit. I would have blamed myself too. It was my fault we were stuck here, with very little hope for the future. But this blame game could have been presented in a more humane way. I'm not saying I was scared he might push me towards the storm. Or maybe, I was!

"You can't talk to him like this fucker! It's nobody's fault. You volunteered to come. Remember? Nobody would be responsible for your well-being. That's what the terms and conditions were for this trip. So stop acting like a pussy and think of something."

It was really sweet of Lily to come to my defense. Somebody was being rational. And it was not me or Aarush. It was Lily. Unexpected, but wonderful nonetheless.

"SHUT UP YOU BITCH! I'VE HAD ENOUGH OF YOU!"

With one loud scream, Sidd answered Lily's allegations with a violent push. Lily stumbled backward. She hit the ground with a large thrust and her face was twisted towards the entrance. Towards the wind. Fortunately, I reacted sharply to pull Lily away from the force of the gusting winds. It was a matter of life and death.

I bet, I would have broken Sidd's 32 white little chicklets then and there itself. But quite surprisingly, I didn't have to do anything. Sidd's bright cheek, decorated with his impeccable jawline met with a tight, yet loud slap that forced his face to take a full 90 degrees turn. And that slap was gifted by none other than his girlfriend, ex, or whatever. That slap was the result of the culmination of the enormous amount of frustration that Purvi had been housing inside her for all these months.

"Listen here Mr.Know-it-all. What did you say? You've had enough of her? Well, guess what? We've had enough of you. Time and time again, you've been an absolute d**k. Do you think you can fool your way around with flying lies? We're not as dumb as you think. The only person who is a real dumb-ass here is you yourself. This slap? It's the least that I could do here in these circumstances. If you really want to complain, go to your bloody Simran and cry your pants off. You bloody coward. You fucking crybaby! You don't deserve me. You don't deserve love. You should live alone. Die alone. I don't care whether this cyclone gets me or not. But it should definitely get YOU!"

There were tears in Purvi's eyes. It seemed like this slap was not just a reflex action for the injury caused to her bestie. It was much more than that. It was a statement from Purvi. That she was not one to be played with. And even though I'm a guy, I was ready to stand with her if any debate ever arose on this issue. Sidd had been treating her like shit. You could notice that in the college premises itself. Every other girl and Sidd would have laid his hands on her. Purvi being an angelic being, was too blind to see this. But finally, her eyes were opening. Was she too late though? To realise her worth in such dire circumstances? Only time would tell. But it's always 'Better late than never'. I had no idea who Simran was. Probably another one of Sidd's victims. Or probably much more than just a victim. But if she was able to make a girl like Purvi slap somebody on the face, she was definitely one to watch out for.

As I mentioned, it was all about calming the nerves and strategizing a way out. With the way things were going, we were not leaving the island anytime soon.

CHAPTER FOURTEEN

SIDDHARTH

Have you ever felt like you've been stuck with some 2nd-level retards? You've no way out, and those people are just there to make your situation even more miserable? Yeah? Ring a bell? Hmm... That's exactly how I was feeling back there inside the cave.

We were trapped inside a cave, which was more like a cage. There was a pretty wide exit that could accommodate all five of us at once. But it was guarded. Not by some random bar bouncer. It was guarded by an invincible force of nature named storm, cyclone, wind, or whatever. We would be blown away into the horizon and there we would be disintegrated into bones and flesh in no time. This cave was acting as an insulator against the forces. But I knew it was not a permanent solution.

Dean was the dean for a reason. He was wise, and at least he knew the stuff he was doing. Not allowing an official trip into this shithole was the most logical thing to do. That decision sounded like music to my ears. But then our wannabe hero Nadeesh decided to pull a rabbit out of his hat and arranged a trip all by himself. As if he was freaking Superman or something. Now when I tried to confront him, I was met with insults from Lily and a thunderous slap from Purvi.

Ever imagined the life of astronauts? The way they feel in space? Or inside a spaceship? Don't get swayed away by movies and get the impression that life's too cool for astronauts. No, it's not. Life is cool as long as there is radio contact with the earth. Once there is disconnection, they're on their own. At an entirely foreign location, without any prior knowledge on how to survive. I'm not comparing our situation with that of astronauts. But even you could strike certain similarities. The cyclone was the open universe. The cave was our spaceship. And we had lost all contacts because our cell phones were not receiving any sort of signal. It wasn't a normal cyclone you know.

While they were discussing what to do further, I was recollecting a story I heard during my childhood. The disintegration of the space shuttle Columbia on its re-entry to the earth's orbit where all the 7 crew members met with a tragic death. One of them was our national hero, Kalpana Chawla. All 5 of us were in line to face a similar fate, albeit for our own carelessness this time.

But something was bothering me even more than my impending death. It was Purvi's slap. While I had been trying my best to remain as stoic as possible, it did hurt, from inside. She was showing signs of eccentric behavior since that day when she asked about Simran. She had known about her. Confirmed by her post-slap lash out. Who told her, I didn't know. And I didn't care to inquire either. Cheating in a relationship should be normalized, according to me. Purvi was certainly not the first on whom I cheated. But it was definitely the first to slap me for that. Either she regarded herself very highly, or it was too tough for her to digest that our dear old Miss Freshers had been blatantly disposed of by her boyfriend unapologetically. Whatever might be the case, she was hurt. Otherwise,

Purvi wouldn't slap someone for no reason. But even though she was trying to heal her broken heart, I felt like our priorities should be shifted towards our lives, not love. That's why I confronted Nadeesh. It was his fault. Whether he admits it or not, it was his fault. And Lily coming out in his defense was pure melodrama. She deserved that push. And Purvi coming out in Lily's defense was melodrama ultra pro max. She deserved much more than a push. I was just not able to compose myself after the slap. Otherwise.......

"Hey, Sidd... Got a minute?"

Oh! Here comes creepy Aarush to disrupt my train of thoughts. The cave had different compartments, storing different tablets and inscriptions. I was seated in the smallest one, which was deep inside the cave, away from the entrance. The compartment immediately following the entrance was the biggest one. That's where everyone else was resting. Well, everyone until now.

"Ya-ya. I've got a minute. But not a millisecond more than that. So, speak up."

I was in no mood for any consolation. I was well equipped to handle my setbacks myself. And I was in no mood to entertain Aarush with the precious little time I had for myself before our death. What did he think? I didn't know? I knew he had a crush on Purvi. One could easily say that from his attitude towards her. And since today's morning, both of them had been sticking to each other like a new couple in love. It was a 'sone-pe-suhaga' moment for Aarush. And an 'ek-teer-se-do-nishane' moment for Purvi. These Meany Little Bastards!

"I'm really sorry for what happened back there. It was unnecessary. But, as far as I know Purvi, she 'll never even hurt a fly. Maybe all she craves for is a little attention.

And to be fair, she deserves it. There are a lot of misunderstandings in every relationship. But eventually all things fall into place. I hope your case follows the same principle. I know you'll find a way."

How dare he? He's giving me relationship advice? I've been with more girls than he's been with books. I've wooed more people than he's ever met in his life. And he dares to lecture me on what a girl wants?

"Oh! Please Aarush! Don't teach me about importance. I know very well what Purvi deserves. Besides, I've saved her life. Putting my own at risk. What have you done? Apart from hopeless stalking, of course."

That was a low blow. He gave a shocked reaction, replaced by a disappointed look and went back to where we came from. Serves him right!

CHAPTER FIFTEEN

LILY

Things were in tatters. And Sidd was only making things worse. I wouldn't blame Purvi for that majestic hit. I knew something was definitely not right between her and Sidd. Actually, a lot of things were not right between her and Sidd. I even cared to inquire back at the station. But she kept mum. So it took a violent push to her best friend to get her talking. Honestly, since that push resulted in that slap, it was totally worth it.

Now then, we have a new person in question. Someone not related to us in any way. Yet she utterly destroyed Purvi's love life. I knew Sidd would mess up. He was a physical, mental as well as and emotional wreck. I had warned Purvi about the same. She was too blind to notice earlier. Now that she had finally broken free of the shackles, I had to make sure she doesn't turn back and move into that shithole again. I had to be with her, all the time. She needed support. And I was definitely not letting that cheat come near her again. We were trapped inside the scary cave. But I was ready to bet every ounce of my strength to make sure that Purvi stayed away from Sidd.

I craved fresh air. Claustrophobia was creeping in from all sides. Venturing out of the cave was never going to be a good idea. So I decided to venture further inside. It wasn't the greatest of ideas either, but the compartments inside the cave were larger than the entrance, or so they seemed.

I was able to spot Aarush on his haunches, leaning against the wall. I sat beside him. A long silence ensued. I was about to break this quiet flow, but he spoke first.

"Lily! Can I ask you something?"

Odd. But I didn't object.

"Yeah!"

"What kind of a person do you think I am? I know this sounds creepy. But please answer honestly. I could have asked this to anybody. But you're the most straightforward person I've ever come across. So, I need the answer to be as blunt as possible."

Oh! Damn, he was right!

"Hmmmmm... You're a sweet guy. I'll give you that. You're smart and intelligent. No doubt about that. You are not at all funny. In fact, you're an absolute boring capsule. You respect people, which include both boys and girls. I appreciate that. You're calm, sober, and docile. Something which is kind of a double-edged sword. You seem like a coward. I don't know why, but you sure seem like one. Andddd.... Yeah, you are creepy AF."

There it goes. Just what the doctor ordered. He wanted a savage reply. He got one. I might sound rude, but the truth is what he wanted.

I was hoping that my reply would catch him cold. But it was the opposite. He just smiled. Which in turn surprised me.

"Thanks for being honest Lily. Thank you so much. Just one more question. Why do you think I'm a coward.?"

He had stressed that bit. Never mind.

"I'm not saying you're a coward. I'm just saying that you look like a coward. I've never seen you take a stand for what's right. You always accept things for how they come. No matter how much you deserve, you tend to settle for less. That's maybe because of either shame or fear. So yeah, that's what makes you a coward."

Another smile, this time a wider one. A grin, to put it in a better way.

"Maybe you're right Lily." He gives out a deep sigh and goes on.

"I've something to confess. Can you promise me that it'll stay within us only?"

A confession? Was he going to propose or what? No way! Me and Aarush... We were miles apart. Besides....

"OK! I promise." Thes words simply flowed down my throat as if I had no control over my speech.

"I... I... I have feelings for someone you know well. I.. I like her from the core of my heart. I don't know whether we'll survive to see another day or not. So, I don't want to die with so many regrets. Please don't tell her. Not until I'm alive, anyway."

Someone I know well? WHATT THEE HELL!! It better not be......

"You mean.... Purvi?"

"Umm... yah!"

I could have slapped him then and there itself. Not for being bold and confessing his feelings. But for hiding them for so long. All this while, I was bickering around because my bestie was being manhandled and manipulated by an absolute bastard of a charmer. And here, one of the sweetest guys I know was suppressing his feelings out of fear or God knows what!

"What!!! But since when?"

"Since our freshman year. I know how this sounds. Absolutely ridiculous. But even you know this. We can't afford elementary-grade jokes at this stage. We are on the edge of the ledge. We don't even know what awaits us tomorrow, provided we survive till then. You're right. I'm a coward. I was a coward not to associate myself with Purvi when I had the chance, even as a friend. I was a coward to let Sidd play games with the girl I love. I was a coward to keep mum even when I knew about the affair of Sidd and Simran since I was a part of the team too. I was a coward not to confess my feelings earlier. I always thought Purvi deserved better. Better than me, even better than Sidd. But I realized that nobody could be better than Sidd. Especially when it comes to me. I can never compete with him. That's why I kept torturing myself with this poison named one-sided love. But, love, in all its forms, isn't a poison. It's a drug. And I'm addicted to it. Addicted to Purvi. Even if a day comes when she won't give a shit about me, I'll still love her. Still love her from the core of my heart. That's what a drug does to you. Either it submits to you, or you submit to it. In my case, it's probably the latter."

Wow! That's quite some outflow. This idiot had no idea what he was blabbering. If only I knew earlier, I could have protected the dignity of the three lovers. Purvi, Aarush, and Simran. It's better late than never. I knew we would survive this. I promise! I'll unite Aarush and Purvi!

I stepped out of the compartment without uttering a word. I stepped out of the cave without reflecting a single thought. I knew it was risky. But I needed some time alone. Especially after an emotional outbreak from Aarush in this already fucked-up situation!

CHAPTER SIXTEEN

NADEESH

Did I just see Lily leaving the cave? What on earth was she thinking? This is a bloody cyclone. Not some solar eclipse. I tried to stop her but she couldn't listen. Or maybe she didn't listen. She just simply stormed off, without a word.

I decided to follow her. As soon as I stepped out, I immediately regretted my decision. My vision got blurred, and My nostrils were screaming for respite. Mighty winds were toying with my hair. Tears were escaping relentlessly from my eyes. To move an inch, took a considerable effort, since I was trying to move against the wind. Splashes of raindrops were trying to injure me in every way possible, warning me to go and hide back in safety. Yet, in this fearsome setting, I was able to locate two young girls right at the edge of the shore.

LILY AND PURVI!

These were out of their minds. I was screaming at them. Sacrificing my alveoli so that they could listen. In Vain!

I tried to sprint. Sprint towards them. It was a stupid idea. I was getting pushed by the wind every single time I tried to disobey it. Putting all the strength I had left within me, I took a few steps ahead. I stopped. Took a breath. Then went on and on, taking a few pauses on the way. Finally, I was just a few steps away from my destination. Just a few steps away from two brainless girls who were sitting idly on the shore like it was some vacation or something. I had mustered up some power in my larynx. I was about to use that when something dreadfully fearsome happened, which caught me by shock.

Lily was shouting something. Then she turned around with nothing but raw fear in her eyes. This time, I gave a 'FUCK YOU' gesture to the wind and sprinted towards her.

"What's the matter, Lily? What happened?"

She didn't reply. She was shivering with panic. She pointed a finger in the direction of the water. Now I realized why she was so afraid. Soon that panic spread like an infection and I was shivering this time.

There was Purvi, in the water, screaming to stay afloat. Screaming for her life to be spared from the ruthless tentacles of the cyclone. Screaming for somebody to listen to her decibels and arrive as an 11th-hour Samaritan. Neither Lily nor I knew a thing or two about swimming. So we just joined her in screaming. Wishing for the same.

2 people were able to hear our screams. They came rushing out for help. Sidd was a pro swimmer. He could save Purvi. But after what transpired between them just a while, would his ego allow him to put his life in jeopardy? After all, swimming at a pool on a sunny day and swimming in the sea on a cyclonic night were two completely different things.

"What are you staring at, Dumbass? SAVE HER!"

Lily shouted at Sidd. He looked at Lily and muttered something under his breath. He looked at Purvi, who was fighting with the waves with every inch of her skin. He offered a feeble smile, which gradually turned into a death stare. Then he stepped back. Slowly at first, then he turned back towards the cave, leaving Purvi in her shambles and struggles.

"What the hell Sidd! Please stop this shithousery Sidd! Come and help her. It's a matter of life and death!"

I tried to infuse some sense in Sidd. But he was too blind to notice the urgency of the situation.

SPLAASHHH!

Just when I turned, I saw two more bodies in the water. Lily and Aarush had jumped to save Purvi.

As expected, Lily was struggling to move around. In a few moments, she'll be in a similar position as Purvi. Begging for mercy from the cyclone and the sea.

Aarush was trying to deliver proper swimming strokes. I'm not an expert at swimming, but one can easily distinguish between a flawless technique and a technique which is poorly executed. Perfect or not, it was working for him. Lily had stopped midway since she wasn't able to brave the wind further down. But Aarush was taking giant strides and in a few moments, he was already carrying Lily on his back.

INCREDIBLE.

He reached the shallower portion where Lily was waiting for him. She shared Purvi's weight on her shoulders along with Aarush and they both swam to the shore. I helped carried Lily on my back from there and we both moved back towards the cave.

Aarush seemed unfazed. He didn't look like he had just saved a life. Sidd, in his place, would have advertised his achievements to the peak of his prowess.

Lily, on the other hand, looked like a mixed bag. She was trying to recover from the shock. But there was a fire burning inside her. Somebody was going to face the brunt tonight.

CHAPTER SEVENTEEN

PURVI

My head was spinning in a whirlpool of dizziness. While I wasn't knocked out yet, but even that seemed inevitable.

I tried to make sense of the surroundings around me, but nothing made sense. Someone was carrying me on the back? Lily? Sidd? Aarush? Nadeesh? I couldn't even recognize whether I was over a guy or a girl. The wind literally knocked the wind out of my ribs. Damn you, irony!

Thankfully though, things became a little clearer once we entered the cave. The whirlwinds calmed down and it was eerily quiet inside. Somebody put me on the ground with utmost caution. I felt better. My vision was starting to improve. Gradually, I was able to recognize the faces. Sidd was observing my face closely with a smirk. Aarush and Lily were shivering with cold. Nadeesh wore a concerned look. A cloud of thoughts started to fill inside my mind. The sea, the wind, the water, the struggle, the impending doom, the savior. This unannounced arrival of this cloud of thoughts was ready to put me into a chain of confusing fragments, but I was saved by Lily.

"MISTER ASSHOLE SIDDHARTH! WOULD YOU CARE TO EXPLAIN YOUR ACTIONS? OR SHOULD I?"

"Help yourself Princy!" Sidd blurted out.

"Fine! So Purvi! I understand that you're currently not in a situation to comprehend things the way I want you to. But maybe you can listen. And all I want you to do is to listen carefully to what I say."

"I'm all ears." I wanted to speak. But my speech betrayed me at the last min. I simply nodded my head. But even that took away quite a lot of energy.

"Great! So here's what happened. We were walking by the shore, in the winds, which was a shitty idea, to be honest. Anyways. We were so delved in our talking that we failed to notice how close we were standing to the shore. You lost your balance at the wrong moment and slipped into the welcoming arms of the sea. I screamed my lungs out for help. After a few minutes, when I thought I was going to die from a windpipe choke, the three of them arrived. I swear Purvi. That was the first time I was happy to see Sidd. Probably the last time too. I thought that his swimming skills would be put into use to save you. I was really really glad. But guess what? Not only did he refuse to help but he walked away as if nothing had happened. Cursing and abusing you on his way. All this just because you slapped him earlier today. He was ready to put your life at stake because of a slap. An eye for an eye, they say? This fucking idiot can take someone's heart out for an eye."

That was quite a rant. Sidd burst into a laughing fit. If all this was true, I didn't know whether to feel happy or sad. I was aware of the ever-increasing distance between me and Sidd. Ever since Simran came into the picture. Ever since we opted in for the trip. Ever since the cyclone hit us. Ever since I slapped him. This sea-saving episode was just another chapter in our breakup story. I was kind of expecting this. Maybe not inside a cave with a very less chance of survival, but nevertheless, I was expecting this. It did hurt. A lot. A lot more than I thought it would. I tried to keep a stone on my heart at that moment so that I won't break down. The stone thing didn't work. But fortunately, I wasn't in a state to weep. I didn't want to show my tears to that ungrateful bastard anyway.

"Aarush saved you. Even though he isn't as professional a swimmer as this laughing hysterical is. 1st-year Purvi. 1st year! He still has a crush on you. And yet you chose Sidd over him? I bet you must be regretting your decision. Now that we're probably trapped till death."

"Lily...What the....?"

"Shut up Aarush!!! If you're too chicken to confess your feelings, I'll do it myself."

Oh, cruel Lord! I would have preferred the cloud of thoughts over this train of revelations.

CHAPTER EIGHTEEN

SIDDHARTH

Lily had spilled the beans like she so often does. Perhaps she considered it an achievement to observe the shocked faces after blurting out a secret. She was successful this time too. The faces wore bewildered expressions. The mouths were yearning for whispers. For a moment, everybody seemed to forget that they were on the brink of the ledge which separates life from death. Everybody was bemused. Everybody, except one. Yeah, that's me.

It wasn't a surprise for me. Not in the tiniest bit. When you are in a relationship with a girl, there are some additional coupons that come with her. Unfortunately, insecurity is one of them. To make it worse, it's mandatory. I had been observing the stray dogs. Those dogs were waiting to bite at the right moment. And Aarush was leading the pack. He was certainly interested in Purvi. I'm not saying he wasn't a nice fellow. His decency is the only reason I'm yet to punch him in his face. He never crossed his limits. Forget about limits, he hadn't even spoken to Purvi properly. Until today. For the first time in a while, I agreed with Lily. There was no point beating around the bush. Aarush likes Lily. The Sun rises in the east. As simple as that. Either it was going to be her, or me, to spill out this secret. It was probably better for everyone that it was Lily and not me. I would have hurt the sentiments of Aarush. Since I had nothing against him in particular, I didn't want to be the villain. Alas! What difference does that make? Nice guys always end up as villains.

"Umm.. Anybody gonna speak?" Nadeesh was trying to ease the tension. Bloody attention seeker.

"SHUT UP!"

Whoa! A chorus of 'Shut ups'. From Lily, Aarush, and even Purvi. So, she had got her strength back then. You still wanna tell me that girls are not overdramatic?

"Yeah, yeah of course. I must say, even I'm surprised too. Aarush and Purvi. I would have never imagined. I mean, not that they'll look bad together. No! That's not what I'm saying. But, to be honest, they are very different from each other. I'm not sure how they would have gelled up. Perhaps, God does everything for our own good. Not that I mind seeing you guys as a couple. But.... Hey!! Have you and Sidd officially broken up then?"

Oh, Nadeesh. He had no idea that he was only making things worse. He was single. And I could clearly see the reason behind that.

"Be quiet Nadeesh! You're not helping."

Oops. There she goes again. Thank you, Lily.

Maybe I should speak after all.

"Ahem! Ahem! Okay. Aarush likes Purvi. And he tells his little secret to Lily. Well, congratulations Aarush! You've made the shittiest decision of your life." I literally clapped to put stress on my sentence.

"I don't care who Purvi likes. No hard feelings, but it's certainly not me. And you know what? I really don't give a shit. And about us breaking up, well, we were never in a relationship to begin with."

"W---h---aatt" Purvi coughed in the middle of that. She wasn't even able to speak a simple 'WHAT' properly. Yet she managed to shout 'SHUT-UP' earlier. BITCH.

"Yes. I'm right. We were never in a relationship, to begin with. A relationship, in my understanding, is a two-way mutual agreement of unconditional affection. Mark my words. TWO-WAY. But in our case, it was always just one-way traffic. Purvi was the one to dictate terms. She would decide our dates. She would decide with whom I should talk. She would decide when I was allowed to go out. She would decide my contacts, my choices and my entire character was being shaped by her only. And it was a character I was beginning to hate. I was slowly beginning to hate myself. And I've never had such an experience before. I'm a guy who loves himself. Who loves himself the most. And no fucking girl in this entire universe can take that away from me. Purvi, you are just a pawn. Simran is my queen."

That look on Purvi's face suggested that she wanted to slap me again. Slap me harder. Slap me with all her might. Slap me with everything she's got. But no. She was able to restrain herself. There was a look of pure disgrace in her eyes. But I'm glad we've got a satisfactory closure. Satisfactory for me at least. And if this was not the fairytale ending she was hoping for, so be it. I had no business keeping her happy. I didn't love her anymore. Not after that slap anyway. She used to be important to me. But she was the one who hurt my self-esteem. And nothing which has some mass and occupies some space has got more value than my self-esteem. Nothing. Not even Simran!!!!!

CHAPTER NINETEEN

AARUSH

I used to be hopeful. In spite of the utter shambles that we were in, I used to be hopeful. I used to believe that we would somehow survive this rampage. We would somehow salvage ourselves out of this. But now, if I was given a choice between survival and doom, I would have chosen the latter without hesitation. Ashamed would be an understatement. I was feeling depressed from within. At a time when I should be feeling scared, I was devoid of emotions. And you know what the worst part is? There's nobody else to blame but myself.

I put my trust in Lily. Even after knowing the fact that she was not good with secrets. I won't lie, but some part of me was secretly hoping that she would tell everything to Purvi. At least my ears would be functional by then. But again, the other part, the shy part, the dominant part was somehow able to convince me that I was stupid to blurb out a long-kept secret like that. It wasn't actually Lily's action or Purvi's expression that hurt me. What messed up the situation was the timing of it. The situation demanded all of us to come together and think of something to survive the night. With the hope that help would arrive in the morning. After all, we weren't stuck alone. We had two high-profile hostages by the nature. Nadeesh and Lily. But instead of acting rationally and finding out a solution, we did something which was the first among the various DON'Ts during a calamity. WE PANICKED!

If only one of us could have restrained his feelings and acted on instincts, we could have been much better off. Unity was the need of the hour. On the contrary, not a single one of us was ready to compromise for the greater good.

I got carried away by emotions and spoke outright at a moment when I shouldn't have. Lily was too blunt to accuse Sidd of whatnot. Sidd, in turn, spoke his heart out. His true feelings. His intentions. Damn! I used to believe that Sidd would be the last person to have a dual personality. He was a straightforward, talk-to-my-face, fire-with-fire kind of guy. But maybe I was a little immature to distinguish straight-forwardness from honesty. And this cyclone, just one isolated evening in this cyclone was enough to thrust me into reality.

Purvi was probably experiencing the weirdest evening, night to be precise, of her life. A dream adventure was turning into a nightmare. First, she was discarded by Sidd during our arrival for his more prioritized YouTube video. Second, she slapped her boyfriend, ex-boyfriend, whatever, out of immense frustration. Next, she almost drowned herself to death. After that, she was trash-talked-to by Sidd. Lily's statement about me having a crush on her, was actually the final nail in the coffin.

I wanted to calm everyone down. I wanted to pull everyone back to the menacing reality that awaited us. I wanted to focus on the situation at hand. All these things would be worthless if we don't make it out of this cave; in one piece and alive. The slightest thought of getting crushed under this cave, or rotting out of starvation, or being blown and thudded away by the storm, or being devoured in one go by the wrath of the sea, or being burnt into a toast by the lightning; these thoughts sent tremors down my spine. And these tremors were starting to increase. I could feel them under my feet. At that point, the perilous realization dawned upon me. These tremors were not inside my head or spine. These felt real. Real in a threatening way possible. The Sky, The Sea, The Wind. They weren't able to completely sabotage our unity. So, they decided to call some reinforcements. Their best ally, The Land, joined the battle. And this time, even a highly optimistic Aarush would have relinquished all hopes of any chance of survival. What chance did I have? The cave started shivering. The voice of the devil started ringing in my ears. It spoke only one word. "DEATH". Cyclone wasn't a new thing for us. We had experienced lots of them before. But we were not prepared for AN EARTHQUAKE. It struck at the right moment. We barely had a few minutes. This cave was one of the strongest one I had ever seen. But to be fair, it wasn't enough to withstand an earthquake.

I sat on the ground for a few seconds. I closed my eyes. I was trying to let go off all the things that happened. A fresh mind was the need of the hour. If we were to survive the un-survivable, we better get things rolling.

I wasn't praying for sympathy. I was praying for a miracle. I was ready to trade my own soul for such a grand miracle!

CHAPTER TWENTY

LILY

I hate to be the bearer of the bad news. But more often than not, this elite responsibility falls on my shoulder. I didn't want to spit everything out in that way. I had dreamt of an evening walk in a park, where I would tell everything about Aarush to Purvi. But I wasn't sure whether we would live to see another evening. To have another walk. To talk again. Besides, the heat of the moment kind of activated the 'Bitch Mode' inside my head. And I would happily embrace that mode if it meant punishing Sidd. I was worried for Purvi. And Sidd just added fuel to fire with his actions. Ego is one factor but how is that more important than saving a life? If not for Aarush, we would have lost Purvi by now. I understand that considering the situation at hand, even our own death seemed very likely, but I would have hated to see Purvi on top of the list. I somehow felt that their breakup was inevitable. #Survi was good only for the audience. Never for themselves. It's for the better only. For Purvi at least. I don't care what Sidd felt anyway.

"Lily! Wake up! For F-Sake!"

Never in my entire life of 21 years, had someone shouted at me like that. It was Aarush's voice. I was asleep. I turned around to shout back at him. But before I could do that, a lump of dust fell on my face. I threw it away immediately, thinking it was a prank from his side. But Aarush is not Sidd. He was well aware of the gravity of the situation. I looked up. I wish I hadn't. For the umpteenth time in this trip, I started getting nervous. But for the first time, I started losing my senses. Cracks were forming at the top. A vibration was echoing through the cave. The cave was shaking, non-stop. IT WAS AN EARTHQUAKE!

"What the ----"

"I know right! Quick, get up and wake everybody else. We have to leave the cave. NOW!"

I hate being shouted at. But I didn't flinch an inch. I woke hastily and sprinted off to do as directed.

It was pitch black inside. The cyclone had picked up the pace. It was howling through its winds. The earthquake played a perfect partner in it. What initially felt like a passing earthquake was just warming up. It was escalating at rapid heights. The cracks widened up. Pieces of stones and rocks started to fall from the ground. We were stuck in a prison of death. Inside, the cave was licking its fingers to crush us under its weight. Outside, the cyclone's mouth was watering to devour us in its tentacles. Cyclones and earthquakes, when combined, can produce the most devastating natural calamity, which goes by the name, Tsunami. It was a word that constantly kept pricking our minds.

"Everybody! Listen up! I know what you guys are feeling right now. I feel it too. I won't lie about it. But maybe you have already made up your mind that you're going to die. Yes, I've too. But since we have got nothing to lose, why not try our luck once? It is futile to remain inside the cave and pray for a miracle. Let's move outside. I know it sounds stupid. But trust me. Being blown away by the wind or being flown away by the water grants you a better chance of survival than being crushed under rocks. But the path ahead won't be simple. Nor will it be easy. Running amidst an earthquake is a suicidal thought. The ground shakes once and you fall down hard on your face. Just at that moment, a rock falls on the back of your head, and BOOM!, you're finished. Before this trip, I had said that even if nobody agrees to go, I'll go. I'm saying the same thing now. Even if nobody agrees to follow me, I'll go alone. Now then, who's in?"

That was probably the worst pep talk I've ever received. But in all honesty, that fired me up. I wanted to join him. Join him for the adventure which had no certainty. Yes, our route to the entrance of the cave might last a few minutes. But in such a journey laden with risks, those few minutes will feel like hours. The Sword of Satan was swinging viciously over our heads. Perhaps it was one last effort from God to save our lives. I was ready to catch this opportunity with open arms.

"I'm in." I put my hand over Nadeesh's.

"Me too". Aarush and Purvi spoke in unison. Then looked at each other and smirked. Awkward, yes. Sweet? Definitely yes.

"Common Sidd," Purvi spoke. This time with a much softer tone.

"Let us everything behind ourselves. We don't even know whether we'll survive to hate each other. So please at least end this on good terms. Throughout this tour, there have been quarrels. Between everybody. Yes, this tour has been a total disaster. But we still have the time to make things right. Please Sidd! For this one time. For this last time. Let's stick together. Hopes in unison are much better than prayers in solitude. Are you in?"

Purvi held her right hand out. Sidd thought for a moment. He looked at our faces. Then, in a surprising turn of events, he shook it. With a smile. This time, a genuine one. This time, not a tiny bit sarcastic.

"Alright then. Here goes nothing."

Nadeesh held out his phone and switched on the flashlight. We followed suit. Even 5 bright flashlights were not enough to light up the cave. But the path was visible. Meanwhile, the earthquake was getting severe. It simply refused to stop. I was holding Nadeesh's hand. Purvi was holding mine. Aarush was holding Purvi's and Sidd was holding Aarush's. We ensured that our grips were tight enough.

"Alright. 1-2-3.... RUN FOR YOUR LIVES!!"

We sprinted off in one go. We managed to dodge a few rocks on the way, thanks to Nadeesh. Our vision was getting blurry. But we managed to notice the entrance of the cave. Hazy, but it was real at least.

"Just a few more steps to go."

I was concentrating on the way. But little did I know that when danger approached, it approached from all sides. A huge rock fell on my back and I fell face-first on the floor. That's it. My doom was nigh. If this is what death feels like, it better be quick.

But no. I wasn't going to die so soon. Not until Nadeesh was alive. He put all his might to remove the rock from over my back. He wanted to carry me on his back but I refused. That would have slowed us down. I got to my feet quick enough and after that momentary pause, we continued to run.

Almost 5 steps away from the entrance.

4

3

2

And just then, a huge tremor came sprawling beneath us and threw us off the ground. The cave started shaking violently and we could hear the alarming sounds of rocks crashing on the ground. Had we stayed inside the cave instead of coming to the entrance, that would have been the end of us. But this situation wasn't too comfortable for us either. Before we could get our posture straight, the rocks guarding the entrance went down fighting. The dome-shaped entrance collapsed and the entrance was blocked with boulders. Impossible for any of us to remove. Impossible for all of us to remove. There we go. Stuck again. This time, surely with a death warrant.

"I promise you guys. I had the best of times with you. Know this"

Sidd was getting emotional. He was in tears literally. All that toughness. All that charm. All that charisma. All those words. Everything dissolved into a pile of horse shit when death came calling. Mr. Perfect was Mr. Crybaby now. If somebody told me that I would feel bad for Sidd ever in my life, I would have laughed at his face. But perhaps I was wrong. I was feeling pity for him. Pity on his statements. Pity on his heavy words. Pity on his ruthless actions. If we were destined to die, along with him, that would be an insult to our personalities.

Nobody stopped Sidd from blabbering. Nobody had any spirit left. Nobody, including me. We were waiting for the entire cave to collapse. Our death won't be peaceful. Our death would be filled with torture. But perhaps we all deserved it. After all, stupid is what stupid does. I was thinking about my mother. I'm she has. The world is a dangerous place for a woman who's alone. Purvi's brother. He would lose his entire family, whatever was left of it, to nature's wrath. The same could be said about Aarush's mom. She would be devastated to lose her husband and her son in a span of a few months. Perhaps she would allow my mom in her house. Perhaps they would run the café together. They won't be happy of course, losing their children at such a young age. But at least they won't starve to death. At least they would have something to distract their minds.

The storm had picked up the pace. The cyclone was intensifying into a super cyclone. The earthquake was keeping up with the cyclone. Both these brothers of destruction had made such an impact on our minds that I was starting to hear strange voices inside my head. Sometimes it sounded like a mixer-grinder. Sometimes it sounded like a motor. And sometimes....wait a second. It wasn't in my head! It was real!

"Do you hear that guys? It's a chopper! It has come to rescue us!"

We were extremely delighted and filled with a new ray of hope when Aarush mentioned the chopper. We started screaming 'HELP' for as long as our lungs could tolerate. We didn't care whether our voices would reach them or not. We wanted to scream. Maybe it was the effort from our side to survive.

The chopper's sound was getting louder and louder, indicating that it was getting closer and closer to us. After a few moments, we were able to hear conversations.

The rescue team started to remove the boulders from the entrance. But even they weren't able to free up the space completely. But there was enough space for two average-sized guys or girls to squeeze through.

"Quick! Hurry up! We don't have much time. This cave is going to collapse anytime now."

Nadeesh was the first among us to make his way out. I was glad. I was glad that his survival was a certainty now. Then he helped the rescue team to pull us through. Me and Sidd were out of the suffocating cave. The fresh air felt like heaven. Even though it was a cyclone, it felt like paradise.

It was Purvi and Aarush's turn to escape. Just when she was about to make her way out, her right foot got stuck inside a rock. Aarush was already out. Purvi was desperately flinging her legs with nothing but despair in her eyes.

"Quick Girl!!! You're gonna die!!" The officials were getting restless.

And then Aarush did something which was equally brave and stupid. He jumped back into the cave and squeezed his way inside.

"What are you doing Aarush? Are you out of your freaking mind? Come back! NOW"

Aarush was in no mood to listen to Nadeesh's warnings. He went inside and manually removed Purvi's feet from underneath the rocks. Purvi finally made her way out.

"Good job boy. Now gimme your hand."

Aarush, with a beaming smile on his face, put his hand through the rocks in order to get pulled out. But Alas! The cave's patience was exhausted. The entire cave collapsed in a thundering wave of noise. In a few seconds, the place was reduced to ruins. To rumbles. To shambles. And it had Aarush buried under it.

"NOOOOOOOOOOOOOOOOOOOOOOOOOOOOOOOOOO!"

Purvi screamed out in a dramatic fashion. She ran to the spot and started removing the rocks with her bare hands. I had never seen Purvi this emotional before.

"I'm sorry girl. We could not save him. But we can't wait any longer. This entire island would be devoured by the sea.

Purvi stood up. Her vision was still fixed to the ground. Had she finally made her mind to go?

"I'm not going anywhere without him."

No, she hadn't. And she wasn't alone. We all joined us. We were not leaving this place. We had to see Aarush. Either alive or dead.

"Arghh Fine!" The pilot sensed it was futile to argue with her.

"Make it quick."

All the rescue officers, alongwith the 4 of us, started searching for Aarush's body.

Our efforts were going in vain. There were thousands of boulders and rocks. We didn't have enough time on our side either. But destiny has its own rules to play games. Out of all people, it was Sidd who finally found him.

"I can see a hand. It's Aarush's hand. Common guys."

We ran to the spot and started clearing out the rocks. Now his entire body was visible. He had injury marks all over his face. He wasn't responding. Tense faces with glum expressions were everywhere. Finally, an official spoke out.

"His heart is beating. But I don't know for how long. He might slip into coma."

There were tears in our eyes. Tears of joy. Tears of happiness. We braved death. We braved fear. We braved life. We braved ourselves.

In no time, we boarded the chopper and took up. From above, we could see the sea gulping down the great island. The end of Madhyasthayi. In front of our own eyes.

I looked at Nadeesh. He was praying. Expressing his gratitude to the almighty for our survival. Sidd had broken down completely. His eyes were filled with tears. An official was trying to calm him down. Meanwhile, Purvi was stroking Aarush's hair gently. His head was on her lap. She didn't look happy. None of us were completely happy. Yes, we survived. But we had no idea what fate awaited Aarush. The guy who traded his life for the life of his loved one.

Epilogue

PURVI

I started the story. So, it's very fitting indeed that I should be the one to finish it. We are going to take a trip up the lane. I hope you guys are ready for it.

5 months later

My sleep was interrupted by the constant irritating sound of my phone. No, it wasn't an alarm. I deactivated that a few minutes back. It was the notification sound. Gosh! I unlocked the phone to check the notifications.

50 messages from 1 chat.

Wow! I knew what chat it would be. My section group, of course.

I opened WhatsApp and pressed on my section group, which was pinned at the top.

There were discussions regarding an extempore competition to be held in the evening. And the chats were basically the summary that I would represent our section as well as our batch. I wasn't ready for it. With Aarush still at the hospital, still, in coma, I was finding it tough to cope with my personal life. Competitions are meant to be attended with a fresh mind. With a soul full of energy. A heart filled with a new zeal and excitement. I had none. My mind was preoccupied with thoughts of Aarush. My soul was feeling incomplete. As if some part of it wanted to stay in the hospital. My heart was filled with prayers.

I decided to call Nadeesh.

"Hello Purvi! I hope you've read the messages. All the best."

"Don't be stupid Nadeesh. I can't do it. I don't even have the spirit to talk. How can I deliver an extempore? Common! You of all people should understand."

"I'm really sorry Purvi. But we don't have a choice. We want to go for the win. And you're the best we have. Don't worry. Just be yourself. Just express yourself. We'll all be there. Now go and prepare. See ya!"

He disconnected the call. Now then. What was I supposed to do? I called the most important person of my life.

"Hey Purvi! I was about to call you. I can understand things are tough. But I know you have it in you to succeed. I'm coming over to your place. Let's prepare together."

"Thank you so much, Lily. You're the best. But I'm not sure whether I'll be able to pull it off. I remain distracted most of the time. What if I feel numb on the stage? What if words don't come to my mouth? What if I break down?"

"Hmm. This is for Aarush. Listen to me. Just imagine Aarush sitting there. Cheering for you. We'll keep a chair vacant for him. So that you can picture him sitting there. You'll feel confident and words will flow seamlessly. I'm coming over. I'm getting something for us to eat. Bye sweetheart!"

It wasn't quite a breakthrough, but it was a good idea nonetheless.

The clock seemed to roll by with lightning speed. In no time, I was inside the college campus. Accompanied by Lily, Sidd, and Nadeesh. Even Bhavna, Drishant, Daman, Akriti, Ananya, Abhishikta, and Prasidh were there. Good gracious! So many people to cheer for a nervous me. The expectations were sky-high. I had a feeling I just wasn't ready for it.

The host announced the rules and the event got rolling. There were 8 participants in total. I was the last to speak. They were given topics like 'Mobile', 'Woman', 'Cricket', 'Rain', and many such random topics.

"Purvi Di! You're next."

I sprang up from my seat. I was greeted with a chorus of good wishes and luck. I walked hastily towards the stage and then I realized that I was simply making a fuss out of the ordinary. I composed myself and stepped upon the stage. The host handed me a slip of paper and asked me to unfold it. A word was written on it. A 4-letter word. My topic for the extempore.

L-O-V-E

Wow! What an attempt to make me sob my heart out.

"You've 15 seconds before you start speaking. All the best."

I didn't 15 seconds. I didn't need even one second. I wanted to finish this thing as soon as possible. I stepped on the podium and looked at the audience. Everyone's eyes were transfixed on me. My group in the middle was rooting heavily for me. I wanted to start speaking. But my worst fear came true. The words simply refused to leave me. I was getting desperate. I couldn't even greet the audience. My face was burning with sweat.

I closed my eyes. I remembered Lily's advice. I looked at her. There was an empty chair by her side. I looked at it and pictured Aarush sitting there. Cheering for me. But not like others. Simply smiling. Expressing his support through his eyes. Immediately, my ghosts started to abandon me. My nervousness was reduced to a pulp. I was getting confident. I gripped the microphone tightly. Lily, you're literally the best. I was ready to speak.

"Good evening, everyone. Honorable jury members, respected dean sir, respected teachers, seniors, my dear friends, and lovely juniors. My topic will certainly raise a few eyebrows amongst you since it goes by the name, 'Love'."

It was met with a chorus of cheers. I continued.

"Now let me ask you. What does love mean? We have different perspectives; we have different visions. Hence, we have different answers. Different approaches. You say, love demands sacrifice. I refuse. I say sacrifice shows love. You say love demands pain. I refuse. I say pain exudes love. You say love demands self-harm. I refuse. I say self-harm intoxicates love. You say, love demands being a goofball. I refuse. I say, being a goofball portrays comfort, which in turn, portrays, love. Now, who's right? And who's wrong?"

A silence, followed by murmurs.

"I'm not right. You're not right. But neither of us is wrong. Love is such a thing that never distinguishes between right and wrong. Love is always right. If it involves self-harm, unnecessary sacrifices, and pains, then please do not call it love. It's something else. But definitely not love. We don't have a thorough understanding of what love means. Millions of poets and authors have tried their best to define love. But none of them found success the way they wanted. Love is supreme. Love exists in heaven. Love exists amongst the gods. How can we expect mortal men to define love? Let me tell you about my story. The one who loves me. The one I love. He put his own life at risk for my safety. He didn't even think once before flinging himself into a cave ridden with dangers. I tell you, that's called love. Why? Because he sacrificed himself? Why? Because he followed the you-before-me principle? No! It's love because it feels like love. We go to extraordinary depths to find love. We imagine a proper love story to be filled with tears and blood. But that is not right. Love can be as simple as a forehead kiss. Love can be as simple as a shying smile. Love can be as simple as an enchanting voice. Love can be as simple as napping eyes. I'm sorry but I don't know the definition of love. But I do know this. You don't need to ask anybody about love. You'll feel it yourself, when it comes calling. THANK YOU!"

I managed to hold back my tears. It was a respite that I didn't sob on the stage to embarrass myself. My performance was met with thunderous claps and a standing ovation from the jury. I was glad. I nailed it. How I wish Aarush could have been there!

The claps stopped. Then continued again. This time it wasn't a chorus. It was individual. Someone was clapping for me even after my performance. Everyone looked at the direction of the claps. I was able to make out a figure. He was a guy. He started moving forward. His features became clearer. Finally, I recognized him. He looked weak and pale. But there he was, right in front of my eyes, smiling, like he always does.

Aarush was back!!

What's Next

So, I hope you liked the story. I hope you liked the book. But the story is far from over. If you haven't completed it yet, then please don't move ahead!

What challenges await Aarush and Purvi?

How will Lily and Nadeesh fare in this budding friendship?

Has Siddharth really changed for good? Or is he planning something sinister?

Who is Simran? What role awaits her?

Uff! Lots of questions. And these shall be answered, in the sequel!

Till then, take care, my fellow readers! And please please please recommend this book to your friends. Social media is a powerful platform, you know. You don't believe me? Ask Sidd!

Ingram Content Group UK Ltd.
Milton Keynes UK
UKHW011126180423
420361UK00004B/459